"I'm known now as Suzanne Dawson."

She managed to keep her voice even and to look into his handsome inscrutable face.

Raoul raised a dark eyebrow in his tantalizing way. "Not regretting our divorce, are you?" he asked lazily.

Suzanne was glad of the sunglasses, which hid her expression. "I liked quite a few men when I married you. But I knew quite clearly at the time that I was not in love with any of them—including you."

"Love can be a matter of propinquity," he retorted. "Put two people together for a length of time and they can grow together."

Suzanne felt herself on dangerous ground. "Not you, of course?"

Nothing had changed, Suzanne realized. Raoul still didn't love her....

Other titles by
KATRINA BRITT
IN HARLEQUIN ROMANCES

Other titles by
KATRINA BRITT
IN HARLEQUIN PRESENTS

Many of these titles are available at your local bookseller.

For a free catalogue listing all available Harlequin Romances, send your name and address to:

HARLEQUIN READER SERVICE,
M.P.O. Box 707, Niagara Falls, N.Y. 14302
Canadian address: Stratford, Ontario, Canada N5A 6W2

The Man on the Peak

by

KATRINA BRITT

Harlequin Books

TORONTO • LONDON • NEW YORK • AMSTERDAM
SYDNEY • HAMBURG • PARIS • STOCKHOLM

Original hardcover edition published in 1979
by Mills & Boon Limited
ISBN 0-373-02305-7
Harlequin edition published January 1980

CHAPTER ONE

By now Suzanne had become accustomed to being airborne. Damascus, Bahrein, Bombay and Singapore had been left behind and soon they would be landing in Hong Kong. The sounds around her pressed heavily on her ears; the continual drone of the engines, the voices of the passengers, the occasional snore from a man behind her, all added to her unrest.

So far she had not been drawn into conversation with her neighbour, a slim young man with a shock of fair hair and a sharply defined profile bridged by dark glasses.

Suzanne had wondered fleetingly if he was someone special since the air hostesses had been very attentive to him throughout the flight. He certainly was not wealthy if his clothes were anything to go by, for his slacks and safari style jacket were well worn and by no means well cut. Below his jacket sleeves his thin bony wrists looked pale and delicate where they had escaped the sun.

She thought he looked strangely pathetic—but then she was feeling pathetic herself. For the hundredth time she asked herself, why Hong Kong? What was so special about it? Why should it succeed in helping her to forget the past when other places had failed? How naïve could one be? Furthermore, to accept an invitation to stay with an aunt of her ex-husband when she was striving with every nerve and sinew to forget him was sheer lunacy. But there it was.

She had never been any good at being on her own, and one could not expect to change overnight. It took time. Transition from a spoilt teenager to an adult had been relentlessly swift and harsh—too swift, too harsh. Her spirit had not been quenched, because she had the courage to face and to conquer adversity, but her slender, pampered loveliness had suffered and the fine high cheekbones of her face had a hollow sharpness.

Suzanne leaned back in her seat to close her eyes, suddenly ashamed of the tears welling up in them, afraid they would spill over and embarrass her in front of her companion. Perhaps he was aware of her need for silence, for he did not speak.

Hard luck that it had to be a man beside her evoking memories of her ex-husband. She knew after they had parted and Raoul had gone back to France that she would have to remake her life without him. At the time she had not cared. She would forget him. She had a doting father to smooth her pathway through life. But Suzanne had not reckoned on her father dying so suddenly, leaving her bereft and alone.

He too had missed Raoul de Brécourt, the only man who could better him in the world of finance. Suzanne thought wryly that few women were able to resist Raoul, his good looks, his nonchalant grace, the mocking humour in his intelligent dark eyes. She had fought against his charm for a very long time. Since knowing him she had seemed to be forever stalking around with a swift outraged tilt to her chin at his teasing and his complete indifference to her charms.

Her first impression had been that he was remarkably good-looking, that he had worn his clothes with an easy grace few could command. Excellently cut suits and expensive silk shirts set off his brown mocking face, his magnificently modelled shoulders, and the lean-loined vigour of his movements. His eyes, black as eyes could be, were set fairly wide apart above a narrow nose with a barely perceptible arch and his mouth, interesting and well cut, had a way of lifting at the corners in derisive amusement.

Her father had been keen for her to marry him since they were in the likely process of merging their respective companies. Raoul, her father told her, had enjoyed the usual affairs—what good-looking Frenchman had not? Also his mother had been English; as if, Suzanne had fumed, the latter made up for everything. But she had not been ready for marriage and Raoul had not been concerned about it one way or the other. He had treated her like the adolescent she had been, bringing her chocolates, flowers and small light-hearted gifts with an amused derision that had made her long to hit him.

Once as he had been turning in at the gates leading to the house in his car she had met him head-on driving on her way out. Immediately she had pushed the lever of her car into gear, forcing him to swerve in order to avoid a colli-sion. Right away he had swung his car round to follow her and eventually had compelled her to stop by forcing her off the road. Then he had sprung from his car with the agility of active muscles and had begun to tell her exactly what he thought of her.

'Do that again and I will give you the thrashing of your young life!' he had threatened in low dangerous under-tones. 'Now get out of my sight before I do something that I shall be sorry for!'

Something had happened to Suzanne in that moment. His nearness had set unknown fires alight inside her. But she had not recognised them as coming from the finer feelings of love. She did now, when it was too late. Weary in mind and body after the death of her father, she had driven herself on afraid to stop, tormented as she was by thoughts and memories of the past.

Impossible to look back and recognise herself as the thoughtless, selfish, carefree girl she had once been. To think that once every luxury in the world had been hers for the asking, and even then she had made a scene when it was not there quick enough. Now she did not care if she had nothing. When her father had been dying he had asked to see Raoul, but Raoul had been away in the Middle East on business and his secretary had promised to pass the mes-sage on. There had been no reply. In any case he could not have come in time. He had settled a large sum on Suzanne after the divorce which she had not touched.

She asked for nothing at all except the strength and tenderness she had once held so lightly. How often had she craved for his arms around her, and it was agony to go to sleep each night longing achingly for his firm mouth on her own. Incredible to recall being utterly unfeeling as she had been when Raoul was hers. How she had hated him for disturbing her from their first moment of meeting! How many times had she sought to humiliate him in company only to have the tables turned on herself. She could never recall the words tumbling from her lips in the heat of her anger. But she did recall the hard, merciless grasp of his fingers. In the end, sick of her tantrums and childishness, he had gone.

Useless to remind herself that she had been an unfledged girl of nineteen when she married Raoul, as inexperienced as he was experienced. During her father's illness she had learned that there were other people in the world beside herself. Fearful of losing him, she had nursed him devotedly, herself going to bed each night exhausted and utterly unable to sleep in case he needed her. Now he had gone, leaving her sadder and wiser, and grown up.

The voice of the air hostess reminding them to fasten their seat belts stirred her into action, and looking down, she saw wispy scarves of cloud floating away over paddy fields, their greenness backed by purple hills. The harbour was crammed with the masts of ships against a backcloth of mountain peaks. The plane began to approach Kai Tak airport, a landing strip cutting across the harbour, and the touchdown was perfect.

It was then that Suzanne saw the young man seated next to her reach under his seat for a white stick. He was blind. Tears of pity welled in her eyes and she turned away hurriedly, realising that he would not have noticed them earlier on. She had learned to count her own blessings by bitter experience in the way one did not forget. She paused, wanting to speak to him, but the air hostess was there to give him a helping hand and she hurriedly joined the rest filing off the plane.

The heat met her along with the confusion and babel of foreign tongues. The formalities gone through, she was on a coach which was to take her to the hotel to meet Jeannette de Brécourt.

She was there waiting in the forecourt, an extremely good-looking woman, slim and rather tall. Suzanne wondered as she waved to her from the window of the coach what magical formula Frenchwomen had for being so chic and feminine. Her eyes took in the smart shantung silk suit, the white turban hat framing a face discreetly made up as she gave an answering wave of an elegantly gloved hand. The heat appeared not to disturb her, but it had never disturbed Raoul, she remembered.

Suzanne suppressed an inward groan and tried to dismiss thoughts of him, but it was going to be very hard with Tante Jeannette around.

'Suzanne! Let me look at you.' Jeannette took her hands and looked her over critically. 'You're thinner, but that hollow-cheeked look gives you a poignant beauty, *chérie*. How are you?'

'Fine, thanks, Tante Jeannette. You look younger than ever,' Suzanne said sincerely.

The older woman laughed. 'I'll let you into a secret,' she whispered. 'I never allow my face to get too much sun. But you are young and do not need to take care of your complexion.' She turned and instructed a Chinese porter to pick up Suzanne's luggage, then thrust an arm in hers. 'I always enjoy this little trip on the ferry. I hope you do too.'

Suzanne looked around at the bustling Chinese porters and breathed in the strange Oriental air.

'I'm going to love it,' she breathed. 'I hope I shan't be in the way. You must tell me if I overstay my welcome.'

'No danger of that. You've changed, Suzanne.'

'I've grown up.' Suzanne watched curiously as the porter reached the ferry with her suitcases.

Jeannette, following her gaze, said hurriedly, 'The porters see to your luggage and you collect it at the other side. You have no boy-friend?'

'No. I'm quite alone.'

'You have all your life before you.'

Suzanne's smile was bleak. She wanted to say, that's what I'm afraid of. What am I going to do with it? But she said nothing, thinking back to the time when she had lost her father. Suddenly the world had become an alien place without him. The thought had occurred at the time that she might just as well be in Hong Kong or any other equally foreign place for all the difference it made to her now that he had gone. Well, here she was in Hong Kong and feeling a little excited in spite of herself.

The breeze lifted soft golden tendrils of hair from her flushed face as she followed Jeannette on board the ferry boat to sit on a wooden seat beside her. As the boat gathered speed to nose its way fussily between junks, cabin cruisers, yachts and freighters Suzanne began to feel that she was indeed in the world of Suzy Wong. Incredible that the twenty-nine square miles that was Hong Kong could hold so much fascination, mystery, romance and excitement. Families in coolie hats waved to her from sampans and fishing junks which provided them with a home and a living. As she waved back to them Tante Jeannette cast a glance her way, and decided that Suzanne was not as self-assured as her sophisticated appearance gave credit for. Her enchanting gold-tipped eyelashes were quivering and her small ears, visible as the bright gold hair lifted, were pink and self-conscious. What an enchanting creature she was, Jeannette thought reluctantly, at the same time quashing the animosity she had every right to feel towards her. In the past Suzanne had given her favourite nephew hell, and for that alone it would be only too easy to hate her. Raoul could have tamed her had he wanted to. Perhaps he had loved her too well or not enough. In any case he was well rid of her. However Suzanne, at the moment, was her guest, and there was something in Jeannette's nature which made it impossible for her to hurt anyone.

Suzanne, loving the feel of the breeze on her face, had lifted it to the sun. With her wealth of golden hair flowing in the breeze, she looked sweet and breathtakingly lovely. Her deep violet eyes had lost their shadows, and Jeannette was not surprised that Raoul had not been able to resist her. At the moment she seemed out of place on the ferry, rather like *une dame inconnue* of another age, a beautiful creature from the spirit world tempted by the beauty of the Orient to explore it. Jeannette hoped fervently that she had done right to invite her to stay with her.

She said casually, 'A friend of mine brought me here and she is taking us back. Her car is parked not far away from the waterfront, so we shan't have far to walk in the heat.'

The ferry boat nudged its way to the jetty among sampans rocking on the water. On Jeannette's instructions a porter took charge of Suzanne's luggage and they followed him off the boat. Spicy smells struck Suzanne's nostrils as they left the waterfront behind and walked along crowded narrow streets to the sound of Western and Chinese music coming from the many restaurants and bars providing every kind of cuisine. The long gleaming car which awaited them was parked in the courtyard of a tea-house inside which families were playing mahjong.

The porter stowed Suzanne's cases in the car boot and she tipped him generously before Tante Jeannette could do so. Then they slid into the back seat of the car to wait for the owner to return from her shopping. Presently a small Chinese figure came towards them from the tea-house to present them with two delicate porcelain bowls filled with fragrant China tea. Suzanne accepted hers gratefully, for the heat had dried her throat.

Jeannette greeted the little man warmly. 'Thank you, Chin Lung,' she said graciously. 'I am just longing for a drink of tea and I'm sure my companion is. So kind of you. May I present Mrs Suzanne de Brécourt, who is on a visit here. Suzanne, my very good friend, Mr Chin Lung.'

Chin Lung bowed his dark head low and gave a wide grin to show gold teeth among the ivory.

'Plees to meet you,' he said, his slanting eyes appraising her. 'Welcome to our island.'

When his white-clad figure had disappeared indoors, Suzanne said,

'I don't use my married name, haven't done since the divorce. I prefer to be known as Suzanne Dawson.'

Jeannette allowed the tea to slide down her long, elegant throat before replying. She did so with a meaning glance at Suzanne's ringless left hand.

'Forgive me if I sound interfering, but I would have thought that the protection of a wedding ring is necessary where you are concerned, *ma chère*. A wealthy, beautiful, single girl is open to all kinds of dangers on her own.'

Suzanne agreed tolerantly. 'I learned that before I was married. I know how to look after myself. I'm twenty-two and over the awkward age.'

Jeannette thought wryly that the girl had never known any awkward age. Her movements, the way her long deli-cate fingers caressed the cup, were poetry in themselves. She had not an awkward bone in her body. She would be as beguiling in a sack.

'You've been abroad, haven't you? I wrote my invitation to you almost a year ago.'

Suzanne nodded. 'Your letter was mixed up in most of the correspondence waiting for me when I came home. I was hoping that you were still here when I replied. It's nice to see you again.'

She did not tell Jeannette that she had been out in un-developed countries with a band of volunteers doing menial jobs in between teaching English for the past year. On re-turning home the need to see someone who had once been family had been so great that she had lost no time in writ-ing to Tante Jeannette.

'It's nice to see you too,' Jeannette replied, and found

that she meant it. 'Living it up in millionaires' yachts, were you? I don't blame you.'

Suzanne concentrated on the last sip of tea in her cup. 'I lived it up all right,' she answered, giving nothing away. 'How is Oncle Philippe?'

Jeannette laughed. 'He's away in the Middle East somewhere on yet another project for the de Brécourt empire. I'm alone again, just as I was when I wrote to you. I was so sorry to hear that you had lost your father. It must have been a terrible blow to you, *ma pauvre enfant*.'

Suzanne drained her cup and hastily changed the subject. 'Why Hong Kong, Tante Jeannette?' she asked curiously. 'You've been here quite some time now.'

'Let's say it's the magic of the island that holds me. I came first with Philippe because he has business interests around the islands, and I enjoyed the novelty of it. I'm glad you were able to come before I leave.'

'Are you leaving?'

'Maybe when Philippe comes back. No doubt, like me, he will want to return to our beloved Paris.'

No mention of Raoul, Suzanne thought, and ached to ask about him.

A boy had come to collect the tea bowls when the owner of the car arrived.

'Sorry I am late.'

The strong clear voice hit Suzanne's ears like a bell as the front door of the car was opened and long elegant legs were followed by a slim body. Wide-eyed with curiosity, Suzanne never forgot the first sudden impact of the newcomer's personality. A white sun-dress revealed enchantingly tanned limbs. The only note of colour was the multicoloured scarf tied around the black hair. Rings on her fingers including a huge sapphire on her engagement finger caught the light as she turned in her seat to gaze with lively curiosity at Suzanne. Her dark eyes, her vivid mouth, the magnetism of her startling presence made her an arresting personality. The thought came from nowhere and was quashed as quickly. How right she would be for Raoul! Now why should she think that? Suzanne trembled and recalled the old saying of someone walking over her grave.

Jeannette was saying, 'Suzanne, my friend Mrs Sylvana Lapport, Italian, married an Englishman, now divorced. Sylvana, Miss Suzanne Dawson.'

Sylvana's dark eyes raked Suzanne's delicate features. 'I am happy to meet you, Suzanne,' she said huskily.

'I'm happy to meet you and to be here,' Suzanne answered gravely.

Sylvana chuckled. 'We are two opposites, you and I—I so dark, volatile and Italian, you so slender, so young, so white and gold and typically English. Would you not agree, Jeannette?'

Jeannette's eyes flitted from one face to the other. She said wryly,

'At least you have one thing in common. You are both divorced.'

Sylvana was not amused. 'I do not think that I care for that, *cara* Jeannette. I do not intend to remain unmarried, and soon you will be saying something quite different.'

Her smile, however, was without rancour as she turned to the wheel of the car. Soon they were travelling through the main thoroughfare of the city, dodging bicycles, cars and pedestrians and weaving around the double-decker buses which ran from one end of the island to the other.

Suzanne glimpsed huge garish Chinese signs, elegant skyscraper hotels and shops crammed with the kind of goods which later would hold her spellbound. Enchanted by the colourful crowds, she found herself responding wholeheartedly to the carefree mood of Hong Kong and to the warmth of Sylvana's welcome. And when Tante Jeannette turned to give her a warm enfolding glance, happiness warmed her lonely heart.

Sylvana was saying, 'I have a delightful house in the heart of the city. It is closed in by high mellowed walls and has a delightful courtyard. I simply adore it. You must come to see it later, Suzanne.' They had slipped into using christian names naturally and it was yet another thing that put Suzanne at her ease.

Sylvana went on, 'Of course it is no way as grand as Jeannette's house on the Peak with its wonderful view of the harbour, Kowloon and the New Territories.'

She tossed a warm smile at Jeannette, who sat listening to her with a look of amusement on her well-preserved face. Jeannette at fifty, but looking no more than thirty-five, obviously valued Sylvana's friendship.

The car was now wending its way to wooded heights. Suzanne drew in great breaths of pine-scented air and had her first glimpse of the house as the car swung off the road to enter a courtyard, an enchanting courtyard of flowering azaleas in pots and little golden bells hung from the eaves of the house to tinkle in the breeze. As they drove through a second courtyard, Jeannette said, 'The house is a mixture of East and West, with the West predominating.'

Unlike Chinese houses it was two-storied, with the rooms beneath the graceful curled roofs both spacious and dry.

A veranda embracing the house led out on to terraces from tall glass doors to give a panoramic view of mountains, and islands set in the China Seas beyond the harbour. Sylvana stayed long enough to allow the servant to take Suzanne's cases indoors from the car, then she had gone.

Sun Yu-Ren, the white-jacketed, smart houseboy, had disappeared in the upper regions and Suzanne followed Jeannette up a short flight of steps from the courtyard to a large, cool room. She looked about her with interest, admiring the beautiful Chinese carpets, the mixture of bamboo furniture and collector's items in dark wood. The light walls were hung with etchings of old China and the comfortable chairs with matching settees had beautiful embroidered cushions in tapestry. Abstract sculptures were set in alcoves and inlaid lacquered cabinets glowed richly in the muted light. In one corner of the room rested a floor vase lovely in shape and design.

Jeannette escorted Suzanne to the rooms that had been prepared for her, a spacious bedroom and bathroom kept cool by air-conditioning.

'I want you to rest, *ma chère*,' she said. 'Sun Yu-Ren will bring you refreshment and then you must lie down for a while.'

Suzanne looked round the room at the double bed hung with a mosquito net, the dressing table, wardrobe and the beautiful satin draw curtains matching the bedspread embroidered with tiny dragons. The floor was polished and the Chinese rugs were in muted colours to match the decor of the room.

'Are all the rooms as pretty as this one?' she asked, noticing that the window overlooked the gardens and the harbour.

'More or less. Raoul bought it on behalf of the company to stay in when the occasion demanded. Accommodation can be scarce in Hong Kong when conventions are held, but with this place at their disposal there is always somewhere for delegates to stay. We have a conference room here and it's a delightful place to relax in.'

Suzanne only half heard what Jeannette was saying; the mention of Raoul had set her pulses racing. There was something potent which emanated from his very name; a force which she could feel even though he was absent.

Jeannette had been speaking rather jerkily. Now she was taking off her gloves and staring down at them thoughtfully. At last she lifted her head and looked directly at Suzanne's charming face.

She said gravely, 'Raoul is here in Hong Kong.'

Suzanne felt every vestige of colour drain from her face and she swung round to gaze unseeingly through the window. Taking a firm grip on herself, she spoke without turning round.

'You might have told me,' she said in a small voice.

'I have.'

'Before, I mean.'

'I'm sorry. Actually Raoul was away when I wrote to you a year ago asking you to come and stay with me for a while. I knew you would still be reeling over the loss of your father. When you eventually answered my letter asking if it was still convenient for you to come, I said it was. I fail to see why Raoul being here can affect you. After all, everything is at an end between you.'

Jeannette had spoken rather stiffly, and Suzanne quelled a shiver as she turned round slowly with her long dark lashes shading eyes which were a darker blue than usual, accentuating the creamy pallor of her flawless skin.

'You're quite right, Tante Jeannette,' she replied in a cool little voice. 'Maybe in time, as the number grows, I shall become accustomed to meeting my ex-husbands.'

'Do not talk so cynically—I do not care for it. I might accept it from Raoul, but not from you.'

Jeannette's voice rasped and Suzanne lifted her small determined chin a little higher.

'Why not from me?' she challenged. 'Why did you invite me here?'

Jeannette laughed lightly. 'My dear Suzanne, why do people invite relations and friends into their homes?—not that this is my home. I wanted your company and I thought it would do you good to get away from the social whirl and relax for a while.'

Suzanne bit her lip. Social whirl, she thought wryly. Parties to her were a thing of the past. All this liberated life of free love and trial marriages had never been her scene. The wild parties had, but she had never stepped over the bounds of decorum. Arriving from abroad and her services overseas, Suzanne had been a very different person. During the past year she had experienced every emotion and had learnt what life was all about. And she had not been lonely. Loneliness was what awaited her in her luxurious home in London. Finding Tante Jeannette's invitation to come to Hong Kong had seemed like finding a gift from heaven.

Now she was not so sure. She had counted on never

seeing Raoul again. Feeling hot and tired after all the
strenuous travel, she decided wearily to stay as long as
politeness demanded, then she would go away putting
hundreds of miles between herself and her ex-husband.

'I'm sorry, Tante Jeannette—I was very rude. Please forgive me.' The sweet smile curving her lips brought a
poignant loveliness to her face, and she went forward impulsively to kiss the older woman on her perfumed cheek.
'Thanks for asking me here.'

Jeannette took her hands. Her gaze was very kind. 'I
am having some food sent up to you and I want you to go
to bed afterwards,' she said gently. 'You look as though a
puff of wind would blow you away. I think it is time someone took you in hand.'

Suzanne shivered inwardly. That was what Raoul had
said. She sank down on to the bed when Jeannette had
gone and lay back to gaze up at the ceiling. At the beginning of their relationship he had come upon her holding a
party at home. Her father had been away on business and
Raoul had been keeping a dark mocking eye on her which
she had bitterly resented. But she had been grateful for his
interference on that particular evening. The party had
been a wild success—and wild was the word, she thought,
looking back. Most of the guests had drunk far too much,
but as their hostess she had been too busy seeing to their
needs to drink much herself. Strolling into the grounds for
a breath of air after midnight, she had been followed by
one of the guests, a good-looking student who had been
airing his views on socialism all evening and boring everyone to distraction.

Finding him suddenly in her path the worse for drink,
Suzanne had kept her cool.

'Hello, Derek,' she had smiled. 'Have you come out for a
breath of air too? Rather stuffy indoors, isn't it?'

Swaying on his feet, he had regarded her balefully.
'You're so right,' he had replied in slurred tones. 'And do

you know why? Because the whole lot of you are stuffy—stuffy with money.'

'So what?' she had replied lightly. 'It's money which has been earned.'

He had gazed with utter contempt closely into her face and Suzanne had stepped back.

'You've never done a day's work in your life,' he hissed.

'Neither have you. So what's the rub? My father has earned every penny of what we spend, and earned it honestly.'

'Good for him,' he had sneered openly. 'How nice to be monarch of all you survey!'

He had gripped her arm painfully, but Suzanne had stood her ground.

'It isn't like that at all. I think you'd better go. I don't like enemies to abuse my hospitality.'

'Don't you, by God! Then suppose I forget our little differences and begin to enjoy myself, eh?'

With that he had hauled her into his arms and fastened his mouth on her own in a nauseating kiss, driving her off the path and into a clump of bushes. Realising his intentions, Suzanne had fought like a wildcat as he forced her to the ground and tore at her dress.

In the violent struggle that had ensued she had fast been losing consciousness when suddenly his weight had been torn from her. There followed a crisp crack on the evening air as a fist came into contact with a chin. The next moment she had been gathered up into strong arms and carried into the house.

Raoul had lowered her gently on to her bed where she had lain with an arm over her face.

'It's all right now.' The deep voice had smote her ears and the bed had gone down as he had sat on it beside her.

It had been then that the terrible trembling had begun and he had gathered her up into his arms. She had been held close in his arms for a long time, with pride the main force in bringing her back to normal.

Coaxingly, Raoul had said, 'No harm has been done. Fortunately I was in time.' Then his voice had changed. Almost roughly he had added, 'Whatever possessed you to go out into the grounds with an oaf like that? You asked for it, you know.'

All her former antagonism of him had risen to the fore then, and she had been aware of naked shoulders above her bra and torn dress.

'Did I?' She had blinked back the tears, a natural outlet for her pent-up emotions, and had speared him with dark blue wet eyes. 'Just as I'm asking for it now, I suppose. Well, I'm not changing one man's arms for another's!'

She tried to wriggle free, to no avail, and he thrust a handkerchief into her shaking hand. Hastily she dabbed her eyes.

'Don't be more of a child than you have to be,' he had said sternly. 'You've had a rotten experience, but I'm not sure that it's not what you needed. You've been wrapped in too many wads of money plus an indulgent father.'

Bitterly Suzanne had thrust his handkerchief back at him.

'You sound like Derek! He implied something like that before ... he ...'

'All right,' he had answered. 'Forget it.' His tones had hardened at the threat of further tears in her voice. 'Get out of the rest of that dress and into bed. I'm going to fetch you a warm drink, then you can go to sleep. I'll take care of your party.'

He had stood up to release the springs in the bed and had looked down at her in exasperation. His dark eyes had narrowed at the familiar defiant tilt in her face, at the militant fine-boned chin.

'If you're not undressed and in bed when I come back, *petite*, I shall undress you and put you to bed myself,' he had threatened.

'Beast!' she had snarled with a childish sniff, feeling very sorry for herself. 'You men are all alike—after one thing, with your one-track minds!'

Raoul had reached the door with a couple of strides and his dark brows had lifted sardonically.

'You're learning,' he jibed. 'Just don't lump us all together, that's all. A girl usually gets the kind of man she deserves. A beautiful little rich girl in her ivory tower puts a man on his mettle. He has to show his superiority.'

'By being a beast!' she cried in disgust.

'No, *ma chère*. By being a man.'

He had gone with a mocking salute, but Suzanne had been wise enough not to underestimate his lighthearted mockery. She was in bed when he returned after giving her time to prepare for bed.

'Your drink, *mademoiselle*.'

To her dismay he sat down on the bed beside her as the springs of the bed gave way, bringing her nearer to him in the hollow his weight made. His lean strong fingers had curled around her own as he gave her the drink to steady it.

'Now drink it up like a good girl,' he said. 'Your party is being taken care of.'

He had waited until she had finished all the hot drink, then, reaching out a long arm, he had put the cup down on the dressing table nearby. Life flowed back and Suzanne had slipped down into bed to close her eyes. If willing him to go away had worked he would have been gone, but it did not. The knowledge that he had done her a great service had damped down the desire for anger within her at his continued presence, and she spoke reasonably.

'Goodnight,' she said in a small voice, 'and thank you.'

'No smile?'

'I don't feel like smiling.'

'I know. I'm not insensitive at what you have suffered, but you cannot go to sleep and have nightmares. The whole incident has to be erased from your mind. There are other kisses besides those of lust. If you will turn your face this way I will show you.'

'I don't want you to show me! Please go.'

'If I go now,' he had promised calmly, 'I shall be back in a couple of hours to find you either in a nightmare or unable to sleep. So you can either have the treatment then or now. So which is it to be? I need hardly remind you that you will be half asleep later, and people cannot be held responsible for what they do in their sleep. Do I make myself clear?'

'Why should you want to kiss me? You know how much I dislike you. I only tolerate you because of my father.'

'Maybe I am insisting because of your father.'

Suzanne's body felt like a huge bruise as the numbness gave way to pinpointing the mauled places on her wrists and arms where Derek had tried to restrain her. At the same time it occurred to her that lying helpless on her back with only the minimum of covering was hardly the time to start another fight.

Raoul took his time bending over her. She had sensed the toughness of his body and she had gone rigid.

'Relax, you little fool!'

But she had remained rigid until his lips had forced a response. Suzanne had been kissed many times, but this was the only time when she had not wanted to move away. Her hands had crept up around his neck and she had swooned with bliss. How long that kiss lasted she could never remember but, recalling it afterwards, she knew that it purged away the nauseating drunken kisses forced upon her by Derek.

It was Raoul who moved away by unclasping her arms from around his neck.

For once she had been speechless. Looking back, she knew that it had been a turning point in her life. It had been hard to believe that the world around her was very much the same as it had been when her father was alive. Nothing had changed except herself. She had flinched away from delving too deeply into the past and how she had changed; it hurt too much as did her own foolishness.

As for Raoul, he was in the past. Now he was here again, back in her life. She wondered if he had married again: the mere thought of it was enough to shake her into action. With a restlessness that was all too frequent these days, she heaved herself from the bed to take a shower and change.

CHAPTER TWO

THE next morning found Suzanne in a torment of doubt as to the wisdom of staying in Hong Kong, especially in a house owned by the de Brécourt company. The thought of being beholden to Raoul in any way was distasteful since she had never been beholden to anyone in her life. It was four years since they had met, two years since the divorce. Married at nineteen, divorced at twenty. She had taken a holiday while the divorce had been made absolute. Sun-bathing and swimming in southern Greece with friends she had told herself that she was well rid of a man whom she had tried to regard as an arrogant bully. He was not, of course, but it had made it easier to hate him. Suzanne bathed and dressed, remembering the extreme poverty of the people in undeveloped countries whose most important need, like her own, was to be loved.

Since they had parted she had seen the wisdom in his protective attitude towards her. Very few of the crowd gathered around her had been true friends. Most of them had been sensation-seekers, adolescents who refused to grow up and face responsibilities. Raoul had taught her a lot of life. She had learned bitterly that one did not love whom one chose, one loved a person regardless of what they were. Suzanne could not put a finger on the precise moment of truth when she had realised her love for Raoul: suddenly it had been there.

Closing her eyes, she stood under the shower in the bathroom wishing that the clear sparkling water could cleanse her of all love for him. It did not work miracles, of course, but she stepped from the shower with the conviction that her weariness of the previous day had magnified Raoul's presence in Hong Kong into melodrama.

Refreshed and ready to meet the new day, she slipped the charming sun-dress in cream cheesecloth over her shining head and shook the golden hair free as though shedding all her inhibitions. The low square neck with its embroidered bodice cut on Empire lines and her glowing skin presented a heartening picture in the mirror. Brushing out the heavy mass of swinging hair, Suzanne wondered how she would behave on meeting Raoul again. How would he behave? How could any future relationship between them be free and easy again after what they had been to each other? But Raoul was not only a sophisticated man, he was French, so he would in all probability shrug those wide immaculate shoulders and look elsewhere. After all, she had run away from him, so who was she to blame him?

She stepped into high-heeled sandals and went down to breakfast. Jeannette was waiting for her on the veranda, dressed in pale green silk.

She said, 'Good morning, *chérie*. I was about to send Sun Yu-Ren to your room with tea—I never expected you up so early. Did you have a good night?'

Suzanne slid on to the chair opposite at the table and shook out her table napkin.

'Lovely, thanks,' she replied, and turned to find Sun Yu-Ren by her side.

'Good morning,' he said, smiling broadly and doing his funny little bow of obsequious welcome. 'Plees, what would Missy like for breakfast?'

Suzanne enjoyed the melon and the delicious Chinese fruits. The thin green tea served in handleless porcelain cups was something one could develop a taste for.

They lingered over the meal with Jeannette reading her correspondence.

'Oh dear!' she exclaimed, looking up from reading a typewritten letter. 'I intended to take you around to see the sights this morning, but I was talked into giving an interview to a journalist from London, and this is the result. She is coming this morning along with a photographer to do a story for one of their glossy monthly magazines.' Jeannette shrugged and waved a careless hand. 'You know the kind of thing, pictures taken in the garden and all the best rooms.'

'That's all right,' Suzanne replied. 'No doubt you have other commitments too, but don't put them off because of me. I do hope my visit doesn't inconvenience you in any way. I can take myself off right away if you wish.'

'You're to stay right here. I've never been interviewed before and you can give me moral support. The whole thing is a waste of time. I asked Raoul to come, but he just laughed it off as being unimportant. Just let them wander around, he said.'

Suzanne relaxed inwardly at the thought that Raoul would not be coming that morning. At least it would give her time to pull herself together. As for the journalist, she would remain in the background while Tante Jeannette was being interviewed, having no wish for any publicity herself. In any case she was no longer any part of the de Brécourt empire, she was Suzanne Dawson and likely to remain so.

'I do hope they don't hang about when they come so we can get it over.' Jeannette refolded the typewritten letter and pushed it back into the envelope. 'I suppose they'll expect lunch. How do you feel about eating Chinese food?'

The frown of apprehension on her face was dismissed on a warm smile, and Suzanne gave her a laughing suspicious look.

'I'm easy,' she replied.

'Which is more than I was when I came here. No one could ever coax me to visit a Chinese restaurant, not even for a cup of tea. Now I love it. But when it comes to food here you can take your pick of American, French, Indian, Indonesian, Italian, Swiss, Japanese, Malayan, Korean, Russian and Chinese.'

Suzanne's laugh came more easily. 'Sounds intriguing,' she chuckled.

They were discussing food in general when the sound of a car arriving brought them to silence.

'That sounds like our journalist friend,' Jeannette murmured.

The next moment a young couple came walking casually through the courtyard. The young woman wore a long print skirt and lace sun-top. Her brown hair, urchin-cut, gave her a boyish appearance as she strolled, looking round curiously at the charming courtyard.

The young man, no more than twenty-five or so, wore a trim beard and moustache. Suzanne watched them approach hoping that they were as harmless as they looked. The young woman spoke first and, on closer inspection, Suzanne put her age at around thirty.

'Good morning,' she cried brightly. 'I trust we aren't coming at an inconvenient time.'

She looked brightly from one to the other, lingering on Suzanne's fair face as her slow smile conjectured.

'Not at all,' put in Jeannette smoothly. 'You must be Miss Norma Reagan and Mr Neil Kilbride. I hope you find your journey worthwhile.'

'Indeed I'm sure we shall. Beautiful place you have here. Big too, don't you think?' Her eyes were on Suzanne as if trying to place her. 'I've seen you somewhere before, haven't I?'

Hastily Jeannette said, 'My young friend Suzanne has recently returned from abroad. As a matter of fact she arrived last evening.'

Norma Reagan hoisted her shoulder bag in place and folded her arms. 'Neil,' she cooed, addressing her companion with a deceptive lightness of voice. 'Where have we seen Miss ... er ... Suzanne before?'

Neil Kilbride grinned. 'Not a chance,' he replied with an audacious look of admiration at Suzanne. 'I would certainly have no difficulty in remembering if we'd met before.'

Suzanne sat motionless. Her hair, a golden halo, framed a small face in which only her deep blue eyes gave colour.

She was recalling her wedding day with no recollection of her part in the ceremony, nor of the crowds who had assembled that day. It was quite possible that this young woman eyeing her so suspiciously had been present. But she wanted no reminder of the past; it was too painful.

Jeannette had not moved a muscle. 'Well, shall we start?' she asked. 'Where would you like to be?'

Her eyes lifted quickly above the heads of her two visitors who were still standing at the foot of the shallow steps leading to the terrace and the open windows. Someone had entered the courtyard and was coming towards them with a long lazy stride full of disciplined grace.

Suzanne's heart dived with love and terror. Her soft pink lips opened slightly, her cheeks changed from a sudden paleness to rosy red. Raoul, her heart whispered. Then she was silently rejoicing that he had not changed at all. He was as slim and virile as ever and much more disturbing now that she was looking at him through the eyes of love. Her heartbeats seemed to echo in her throat.

'Be a dear, Suzanne. Go to the kitchen to ask Sun Yu-Ren to make fresh tea.'

For a moment she turned and looked vacantly at the older woman as her words registered. Then, forcing herself back to normal, she rose and sped away into the room behind her to the kitchen.

'Bless you, Tante Jeannette!' she breathed. How kind she was, withholding her full name from the Reagan woman and now giving her time to pull herself together at Raoul's unexpected arrival. At the louvred kitchen door, she paused with a hand on her wildly beating heart. But after giving Sun Yu-Ren the message she felt her courage running out. She simply could not meet Raoul. Running to her room, she sat down on the bed and tried to see some way out of seeing him.

One thing was certain. She could not stay in her room, as Tante Jeannette would be certain to give Nora Reagan and her companion the run of the house. They might come to photograph her room. Standing up, she straightened her dress, used a touch of lipstick and smoothed back her hair from flushed cheeks. There was not a sound as she opened her room door. Sun Yu-Ren had served tea by now and everyone would be drinking it. Why not go through the kitchen quarters and make her way outside?

'Wrong way as usual, Suzanne.'

The familiar deep voice smote her ear like a gong. She swung round at the kitchen entrance to find Raoul behind her. She looked up at him and thought rather dazedly that his black hair looked thicker and springier, and his face a shade paler than the heavy mahogany tan of yesteryear. His well cut mouth looked a little graver than she remembered, but he favoured her with the old baffling expression.

It was the look that had always put her on her mettle. She smiled.

'Hello, Raoul. How are you?'

Her cool little voice brought a spark to his dark eyes which went in the next moment. She moved back a step away from the brooding darkness of his face—an unconscious movement of self-preservation since her love for him was stronger than herself and beyond the bounds of controlled emotions.

'I'm fine. Why did you not come back to the terrace? We were waiting for you.' His glance sharpened. 'What have you been doing with yourself? Have you been ill?'

'No, I haven't.'

'What happened? Was the trip abroad not what you had hoped for, or are you pining for a lover you left behind?'

'It wasn't like that at all—and how did you know about it?'

His eyes narrowed on an instant's pause. 'How does one hear such things? Another of your harebrained schemes, was it?'

His tone, a domineering one, which she thoroughly resented since he was assuming rights he did not possess, brought out her flippant side.

'Maybe I wanted to get right away to think things out.'

'And did you . . . think things out?'

'Sort of.' Despite her determination to keep cool in his presence, Suzanne felt suddenly weary, no match at all for his keen perception. The hand she lifted to push back the gleaming hair from her forehead shook a little. 'Now, if you've finished your cross-examination shall we return to the others?'

Raoul said, 'Our visitors won't be here long, so bear up.' He guided her back to the terrace. His voice and manner had altered. How gentle he could be when he chose. But Suzanne did not want his kindness, for kindness from him was like taking an unfair advantage of her reeling emotions.

They had almost reached the terrace when Raoul spoke again. 'I am sorry about your father,' he said. 'I was very fond of him.'

Suzanne did not look up. She bit hard on her lip to prevent her from blurting out, 'Was that why you didn't come to see him before he died?' But she did not answer. She wanted to go home. Meeting Raoul had been more distressing than she had imagined it would be, and she was in no mood for this which was in no sense a party, but just a small group of people sharing polite conversation over tea.

Tante Jeannette greeted them warmly. 'So there you are, Suzanne—Raoul. Do sit down and take tea. You will find it refreshing later in the heat.'

Neil Kilbride jumped up to pull out a chair for Suzanne and Raoul lowered his long length on the chair beside her. Jeannette passed them tea and Norma Reagan cried:

'You have a beautiful place here, Monsieur de Brécourt. Perhaps you'll favour us by posing for photographs during the filming?'

Raoul shook his dark head and drank the rest of his tea. 'I'm sorry, but I have an appointment very soon, so I'm sure you will excuse me.'

Norma Reagan did not bother to hide her disappointment. 'Not even one teeny-weeny one?' she wheedled with a crestfallen expression on her face.

Raoul shook his head, refused to have his cup refilled and in passing it to his aunt leaned a little over Suzanne to do so. Trembling at his sudden nearness, she drew back, and as she did so her cup slipped sideways from her nervous hand to fall between her and Raoul. They both dived to save it from crashing on the terrace and Raoul closed his long lean fingers over hers as they caught it together in mid-air.

'Sorry,' Raoul said.

'My fault.' Suzanne drew her hands away from his and handed the cup to Jeannette, furious with herself at her clumsiness and with embarrassed colour flooding her face. Pity it had been empty, otherwise she would have been able to leave in order to mop up the spilled tea on her dress. As it was she had to face a barrage of eyes, or so it seemed. Meeting Norma Reagan's curious gaze, she went shivery inside. Was the girl aware of her embarrassment or did she remember that Raoul had once been her husband? Would she discuss it later with Neil Kilbride and laugh because it was obvious that poor little Suzanne had a crush on her ex-husband?

Raoul appeared not to have noticed anything amiss with her, for he left them with a murmured excuse and went indoors. Norma Reagan and Neil Kilbride reluctantly rose from their seats in the sun and decided to begin with the garden. ·

Jeannette said, 'I shall be taking our guests around the house to explain a few things, so you are free to do what you like until lunch, *ma chère* Suzanne.'

It was the escape Suzanne had been wanting so desperately. All the same she hesitated, remembering that she was in a strange country.

Perhaps Jeannette noted her lost look, for she added kindly, 'I'm sorry that my car is not available, but we are not far from the main road and the trams are really efficient and regular. Keep within range of them, though, won't you, if you go out?' Her manner was dismissive as if she wanted her guest out of the way—of what—awkward questions from the two young people photographing the house and grounds? Suzanne did not blame her for not wanting her nephew's ex-wife to enter into the family again. She knew Jeannette would be worried still more if she knew the effect Raoul's strong brown fingers had during the earlier incident of the dropped cup.

Suzanne had felt the contact like a tiny electric shock. On the way to her room she was able now to analyse her emotions calmly, to wonder at the effect he could have on her against her will. The trouble was that she must deliberately deny the call of her heart, which she realised with such bitter humiliation she was capable of following against every instinct of her pride.

Coming lightly downstairs again after calling in her room for her handbag, she unexpectedly ran into Jeannette with the two journalists in tow.

Norma Reagan said with a sweet smile, 'What about posing for us in some of the photographs?'

Neil Kilbride seconded her enthusiastically. 'Please do, Miss Suzanne. Nothing like a beautiful girl for livening up the pictures!'

Suzanne tightened her hold on her bag. Tante Jeannette, she could see, was dismayed at the thought—which made two of them, she thought bitterly.

'Sorry to barge in, but you will have to come now, Suzanne, if I am to give you a lift into town.'

The deep brown voice came clearly from where Raoul stood looking up at them from the doorway of a room near to the foot of the stairs. Suzanne could only think how strange it was that from her first meeting with Raoul she had sensed some link between them; like an inner sense warning her of his presence. Suddenly she felt oddly calm. She even managed to smile down into his handsome, inscrutable face.

'I'm quite ready,' she answered, accepting the inevitable.

As she went down the stairs on winged feet Norma Reagan called, 'Take care! They say it's bad luck to pass people on stairs.'

'You didn't want your photograph taken, did you?' Raoul asked casually when they had left the house behind and the long nose of the car was feeling its way through the mêlée of humans and wheels. Moving bicycles caught the rays of the sun as together with pedestrians they miraculously moved out of the way.

Anger and something much more painful stabbed Suzanne sharply.

'No, I certainly did not, neither as your ex-wife or as Suzanne Dawson—which I now prefer to be known as.'

He raised a dark brow in his tantalising way. 'Not regretting our divorce, are you?' he asked lazily and unexpectedly.

Suzanne started. She was glad of her sunglasses which had been a fortunate afterthought. 'I liked quite a few young men when I married you. But I knew quite clearly at the time that I was not in love with any of them, including you.'

'Love can be a matter of propinquity,' he retorted. 'People can grow on one even when they are absent. Put two people together for a length of time and they can grow together. Not all of them would fall in love, but some would come uncommonly near to it.'

Suzanne felt herself on dangerous ground. 'Not you, of course. You would see what you wanted and take it, which is why you're at the top of the tree.'

'How right you are—but even I can make mistakes. Fortunately I see most of them in time and cut my losses.'

Suzanne's gaze was fixed on his quiet, light hands on the car wheel. Her heartbeats sounded uncommonly loud and she moved away from his arm, which was like a bar of unyielding iron.

'Congratulations on being able to view life so clearly. It must be cosy from that throne of yours to see other lesser mortals going wrong,' she said.

He turned, grinned whitely at her, then gave his attention once more to his driving. He looked lazily uncaring and infuriating.

'Don't you think we ought to bury the hatchet?' he suggested suavely. Another of those quick wicked glances and he added, 'It would never do for us to give the impression that we are still husband and wife. Would you not agree?'

Suzanne tried to tell herself that she was not in love with him at all. What she was feeling was mere infatuation for the French side of him because he was different—the black hair curling attractively in the nape of his brown neck, the near-black eyes that sparkled so devilishly spoke of his French origin. He had learned the lessons of life and had come out unscathed, which was more than she had done. He had shrugged her out of his life as if she had never been in it. Why not do the same?

This strange new country was hers to explore. It seemed fated for her to do so with Raoul. As if aware of her gaze he turned his head slowly and she returned his smile. A strange mounting excitement took possession of her, appealing to her sense of adventure. Where it would lead her she neither knew nor cared at the moment. All that mattered was that Raoul was beside her. He might not be meant for her nor she for him, but nothing could take away this strange new emotion which poignantly held very little pleasure and too much pain. At the moment it was part of the strangeness of the beauty of her surroundings and definitely part of the new Suzanne slowly coming into being.

They were nearing the main thoroughfare of the city where trams raced between a mêlée of traffic and all around was life, bustle and spectacle. The very air breathed with Oriental romance and to Suzanne it represented all the magic of the East.

Raoul began to slow down. He said, 'I have to leave you now while I go on some business. I suggest you stay in the main road here and browse among the shops. The post office is quite near, so you will be able to buy stamps and post your letters and cards. I will meet you there in an hour and we'll have lunch.'

Suzanne looked at him dazedly, at the tanned face with

contrasting white teeth and dark eyes that still held the magic of a person beloved. Even now she could not believe that he was here taking charge of her as he had done in the old days. But it must not be allowed to go on. Funny that it should take her two years to realise that he was the one man in the world for her and that now she had to rid her head of such an idea. How long it would take, Suzanne had not a clue. She only knew that they must not grow any closer for her own sake. The tie between them must be broken if it took the rest of her life.

She said defensively, 'Tante Jeannette will expect me back for lunch, so I'll say goodbye. I shall enjoy looking around the shops and I can take care of myself.'

'I said I would pick you up for lunch in an hour. You are in a strange country and this is not London. Tante Jeannette will expect me to look after you and take you out to lunch,' he insisted.

He had leaned across her to open her door and paused with long fingers on the catch. Suzanne drew back in her seat, finding him much too near. That faint aroma of sandalwood soap, the smooth texture of his clean-shaven face was all too familiar and reminded her of more intimate moments with him in the past.

Again her weapon against him had to be anger. 'I won't have you putting yourself out for me,' she cried. 'I told Tante Jeannette the same. I don't know if you know that her invitation to me to stay with her is twelve months overdue. I certainly didn't expect to see you here.'

Raoul moved so that he was half facing her and let out a short rasping breath. 'What is it about you that makes me ache to spank you? I know you've no time for me, but I happen to know what a little idiot you can be in assuming that there is no harm in anyone. You have to be protected against yourself. You came here and you have to abide by the consequences. Why did you come anyway?'

She said stiffly, 'I came here because I couldn't face London again without my father. I felt that I needed a—a

break, if you like. The year I spent abroad taught me a lot
about independence, but it was different when I got home.
Oh, don't get me wrong—I love my independence. It's just
that I've never known a world without my parents, and it
takes some getting used to.'

Raoul said roughly, 'Clinging to Tante Jeannette won't
help. What you need is a husband.'

'I tried that once and it was a disaster, as you know.
When someone holds out a hand at the time when you're
desperately in need of one, you take it.' Her low tones were
not quite clear as she talked with bent head. 'Tante Jeannette offered me a sanctuary which I don't intend to abuse.
I shall return to London eventually.'

'Then let's make sure you are all in one piece when you
do so. I shall pick you up in one hour from now at the post
office, and you had better be there. And just to keep the
books straight, you are not putting me out. I happen to
be eating with a friend, so we shan't be alone.'

His face when she looked up was handsome in its ab-
sorbed arrogance and dangerously close. Suzanne's heartbeats quickened as he seemed to pause again before opening her door. Her legs were trembling when she stepped
out of the car and she gave him a half smile.

It remained woodenly on her face. Raoul made her feel
all kinds of—emotions. In his company she seemed to run
the whole gamut of them including unrequited love, for it
was clear that he now regarded her as one of his few mistakes—the ones that he wrote off without a qualm. And how
dared he make her out to be some kind of witless fool in
need of protection! A husband, he had said. Well, her life
with him was not the only reason she had learned to quell
sudden impulses and to dissemble. Some of the young men
she had met at her parties and in the course of her daily life
had been the means of teaching her the way of life of the
present day. But she had not been her father's girl for
nothing. He had been a good man and a good father, and
she would never let him down.

Exasperatedly she watched Raoul slide away in the big opulent car to nose his way into the stream of traffic and vanish. The next moment he was forgotten as she wandered past shops crammed with luxury goods like watches, pearls, cameras, diamonds, ivory, jade, silks, porcelain, crystal, coral, leather and beautiful carpets selling at free port prices. Unlike the U.K., the shops would be open at all hours, gleaming in the darkness later like Aladdin's cave of treasures and delights.

Suzanne had never seen anything like it and her slim brown legs moved lightly along on a wave of pleasure. One could spend months browsing around, she thought, recalling the ladder-like streets, narrow, mysterious and excitingly wending their way heavenwards, which she had glimpsed on her way to Tante Jeannette's house. The jade bracelet was exquisite and she had to go into the shop to ask the price of it. It looked at her invitingly from the window of the shop, as did the matching earrings. The shopkeeper smiled at her and said he would certainly take the bracelet and the earrings from the window for Missy.

They were even nicer at close quarters, the bracelet beautifully carved and the earrings enchanting. Tante Jeannette would love them, Suzanne was sure, and she was about to ask for them to be wrapped up when the sound of a clatter outside the shop made her turn her head in that direction.

Through the open doorway she saw the bent figure of a young man searching round for something he had dropped. Suzanne stared, recognising him as the blind young man who had sat next to her on the plane on the way over.

With a murmured excuse to the shopkeeper she ran to the door and picked up his white stick. Then reaching for his hand she put the stick into it.

'There you are,' she said. 'Are you alone?'

The young man stared in her direction without focusing her and Suzanne was surprised how frail he looked. His thin face was ashen and he looked ill.

'Are you all right?' she asked anxiously.

But he seemed not to hear her words. His delicately veined forehead was wrinkled in the effort he was making to remember something. Then he smiled.

'You are the pretty girl who sat next to me on the plane, aren't you?' he said.

Suzanne said in surprise, 'But how can you remember me and know what I look like if you can't see?'

'I can see blurs of colour, and there was a certain fragrance about you that told me quite a lot. Would you mind telling me your name?'

'Suzanne—Suzanne Dawson. Now tell me yours.'

'Alan Edge. Thank you, Miss Dawson.'

A shaft of sunlight had fallen across his face. He looked drawn and pinched, and Suzanne thought his languid look was more than the heat. Something was bothering him, and she wished futilely that she had been more friendly with him on the plane.

'I happen to be doing a bit of shopping,' she said warily. 'Can I be of help to you in any way? I think you're very brave to come here alone.'

He waved a thin bony hand. 'I'm on my way down to the docks, so I won't keep you,' he said.

'Oh, but you're not keeping me. As I said, I'm shopping before having lunch with a friend. I'll come down that way with you—although I'm not sure of the way,' she laughed. 'Anyway, we shall get there quicker if I come with you.'

He hesitated, seemed about to refuse, then accepted her offer to accompany him with a smile. Suzanne took his arm and they walked for some distance while she looked for landmarks she had seen during her car drive from the courtyard of Chin Lung on her arrival the previous day. Keeping her fingers crossed, she blessed her lively curious mind for imprinting the landmarks so clearly on her memory.

Suzanne took his arm and they moved between the crowds on the congested pavements.

'I suppose you have a guide dog back home,' she said cheerfully.

'No. The accident to my eyes happened while my ship was stationed here in the harbour,' he explained. 'It was a slight explosion in the engine room. I took the full force of it. I'm engaged to be married and my fiancée Jane was in Singapore at the time with a dancing troupe. She was on her way here when she heard about the accident, but I was sent to hospital in the U.K., so we missed each other.'

'Tough luck,' murmured Suzanne sympathetically. 'Is Jane still here?'

'I don't know. The explosion was not too serious and my ship left the island after repairs. I've made enquiries, but so far there's no news of her. I've even contacted the police, but they can't do much. The number of people who go missing here is fantastic.'

Their surroundings were taking on a new face, a plethora of warehouses and seedy joints leading to the docks and ferry. But Alan assured her that he would be all right on his own.

'No need to come any farther,' he said. 'Thanks for your help. I can manage on my own now. Thanks a million!'

CHAPTER THREE

RAOUL was waiting for her in his car by the post office when she arrived with a high colour.

'Sorry,' she said rather awkwardly. 'It was later than I thought.'

'I've only this moment arrived myself,' he admitted in clipped familiar tones. 'You look warm.' He opened the car door for her to slip in beside him and she shut it hastily herself to save him bending over her to do it.

She sighed with pleasure. 'I love the warmth of the sun. I feel like a ripening peach. Lovely feeling!'

His dark eyes flicked lazily over her glowing face, a glance that made her colour deepen still farther.

'A peach has a heart of stone,' sardonically. 'Is that what you would have me believe about you?

His mocking look was more marked and she knew he had guessed that her hasty action of shutting the car door had been done with a purpose.

'I don't care what you believe about me.'

'No?' He started the car and slipped easily into the traffic. Then, 'How is it you came to Hong Kong alone? I cannot imagine you as a loner, and I am sure you would never regard yourself as one. Do you?'

Suzanne stared through the windscreen and her voice hardened slightly.

'Does it matter how I regard myself? In any case, it isn't any of your business, is it?'

'Let us say that like all men of experience I have a weakness for trying to help the unfledged. Especially you. You are an odd product of a doting father who has always protected you against the deeper emotions and sharp corners of life. *Pauvre enfant*, with so much to learn the hard way.'

40

Suzanne lifted her chin militantly in the knowledge that Raoul would recognise the old familiar gesture against his mockery. But he did not see it. The crowded road ahead demanded all his attention. She bit her lip, knowing that her wit was no match for his cynicism. But she tried.

'I'm a fast learner,' she said. 'I had a good teacher—you.'

'I learned something from you too,' he returned. 'Does that surprise you?'

'It certainly does. Whatever could I have taught you that you didn't already know?' she asked with mock modesty.

'Not taught me,' he corrected. 'I learned something about you, which is a very different thing.'

'Really? Do tell me.'

He grinned at her look of quelling disgust, then gave his attention once more to the road ahead before he began to speak.

He said audaciously, 'I will begin with the nice things about you. I discovered that your figure is really as perfect as it appears to be, and that those absurdly long eyelashes are as naturally gold and silky as your long flowing hair. You are a bit too thin at the moment, though.'

'Thank you!' she cried indignantly.

'But this is the rub,' he went on. 'Your fine-boned, delicate appearance is misleading. That creamy un-blemished skin, those pink lips are the result of robust health. You might possess delicate wrists and ankles, but you are disgustingly strong and healthy.'

Childishly she snapped, 'Pardon me for not being on my back in some hospital!'

But Raoul did not appear to be listening. He swung the car off the main highway and drew up at a high wall practically in the heart of the city. The warm air hit Suzanne's face like an oven as she stepped from the car almost with a feeling of claustrophobia at the tall buildings surrounding them.

As she looked around her helplessly, Raoul took her arm

to lead her to a heavy wooden door in the high wall. It opened easily to reveal a delightful courtyard and a Chinese-style one-storied house with curling roofs. The fragrance of mimosa and frangipani drifted on the warm morning air from ornamental tubs set around the tiled court and chairs were set beneath the shelter of the veranda.

Sylvana Lapport descended upon them rather like a bird of the tropics in her blue silk kaftan and Suzanne saw Raoul step forward with a sudden awareness.

'So here you are, Raoul, and you have brought Suzanne as promised. How clever of you to come just as lunch is ready,' she cried, offering her long slender hands to them with expressive gestures. Her dark eyes glowed and to Suzanne, still teetering over her surprise at meeting Sylvana again so soon, the effect was almost theatrical.

There was an elusive hint of perfume as she linked both their arms and walked with them into a cool bright room.

'Do sit down, *cara* Suzanne. Raoul will pour the aperitifs. I hope you like Italian food. Excuse me, won't you?'

Sylvana motioned Suzanne to a small dining table already set with bright mats, silverware and sparkling glass enlivened by a flower arrangement in the centre, then left the room.

Raoul served the drinks from a glass cabinet for all the world as if it was his own establishment. Uneasily, Suzanne wondered if Sylvana inwardly resented her being a third party at her lunch with Raoul. Looking around the cosy room it was easy to picture them together and Raoul handing Sylvana a drink as he was now handing one to herself. She noticed that he had remembered her preference for non-alcoholic drinks, and she murmured her thanks for the tomato juice.

Sylvana had obviously prepared the meal herself, for she carried it in with no sign of servants about. She had evidently gone to great pains to present her best culinary offer, because the meal was deliciously prepared and presented. But Suzanne might have been eating sawdust from the way it stuck in her throat. She felt de trop, an intruder into what had been intended as a meal for two.

For some reason Sylvana disturbed her almost as much as Raoul. She knew a sense of disquiet until Sylvana's husky voice aroused her. She had handled the situation superbly, whisking off one course to replace it immediately with another equally delicious one.

'How do you like Hong Kong, Suzanne?' she asked, popping an olive into her mouth and smiling at her across the table.

'I like it very much,' Suzanne replied rather inanely.

'I love it here. Life is never boring. There is so much to explore, and the different kinds of food are an adventure in themselves. Then, of course, the people have something to do with it,' her hostess cried warmly.

Sylvana picked up her wine glass and sipped the last of it, glancing across the table at Raoul as the liquid slid down the slender throat. Catching the look between them, Suzanne squirmed inwardly as her thoughts tormented and nagged. What was the relationship between them? How much had they been or were now to each other? Futile to ask in any case; it was none of her business.

Raoul's attractive mouth curved slightly upwards at the corners as he eyed his hostess with a faintly cynical and affectionate regard. He lifted his glass in a kind of mock salute to her.

'Long may you stay. I have yet to find a better cook and more beautiful hostess,' he drawled.

'Is that all?' Sylvana pouted beautifully.

'It will do to be going on with,' he replied, and rose lazily to his feet. 'And now I'll make the coffee.'

He collected the dishes, reached for the tray nearby and carried them away. Again Suzanne had the feeling that he belonged here in this lovely little Chinese house. Was that the reason why Sylvana had no servants? There was no one to pry. Then she dismissed the thought as unworthy, at Sylvana's next remark.

'I have a woman in each day to do the household chores,' she explained. Her sudden smile was warm, as she added, 'That was in case you offered to wash the dishes. You know, I have been longing to meet you.'

Suzanne gazed frankly into the dark eyes. 'You mean you knew about me?'

'But of course. Come, let us sit on the terrace for our coffee.' Sylvana led the way to comfortable white cane chairs heaped with cushions in the cool of shade, and sat down gracefully. 'Make yourself comfortable.'

Suzanne sat down like one bemused, wondering how much this fascinating creature knew about her. It was very disconcerting to meet a stranger who presumably knew all about her—or as much as Raoul and his aunt had confided. From Raoul, she was certain that this was not much. As for his aunt, Suzanne was not so sure.

Sylvana was studying her quietly. 'You are quite a surprise and not at all the kind of person I would expect Raoul to marry. You are so English, so beautifully slender with so lovely a complexion, almost like a doll. And you look so young. I expected someone older.'

'I'm twenty-two.'

'Ah, but younger still when Raoul married you. He is a man of the world. He has known many beautiful women.'

Suzanne was faintly annoyed. She had not come to lunch for a post-mortem on her marriage and she had not asked for Sylvana's opinion, which the latter seemed bent on giving. So she gave her companion no more than a slight interest. It was her only defence against the hurt which the woman's words, however unintentionally, were inflicting.

'I was with him often when he met those beautiful women. But he married me,' she said composedly. 'In any case, it's all over. I don't wish to speak of it at all. Don't misunderstand,' hurriedly. 'I appreciate you being so frank with me. But as one divorced woman to another, I don't think we need discuss our former marriages, do you?'

Sylvana's dark eyes deepened in colour, then she laughed merrily.

'You and I are going to be great friends—I feel it in my bones.'

The sapphire ring shone in the beam of sunlight as she leaned forward to pat Suzanne's hand.

'What joke have I missed?'

Raoul came striding forward bearing the coffee on a lacquered tray which he set down on the glass-topped table and proceeded to serve it. He looked handsome, uncaring, and he had come back into her life as if he had never been away. If only he was not there to keep alive the memories that she wanted so much to forget!

Sylvana was giving her full-throated laugh. 'No joke, darling. Just woman talk.'

The endearment seemed to echo on the morning air to Suzanne, and Raoul took it as a matter of form. Sylvana reached for a cigarette box beside the tray on the low table, extracted a cigarette while Raoul obliged her with a light from his pocket lighter. Suzanne had refused, but she was aware of Raoul lighting one for himself.

As he leaned back lazily against one of the veranda posts to stare out over the tiny courtyard, Suzanne found herself wishing that she was older. In those first moments while they drank their coffee she felt again that she was the last guest outstaying her welcome. Sylvana and Raoul were not of her world. They belonged to a much more advanced one.

From where she sat Suzanne could not see Raoul's face, only part of one broad shoulder. He stood very still. In repose he maintained the same disciplined grace that marked every movement. He had never seemed tired nor to flag his energy down after the most energetic day, Suzanne remembered.

The coffee was delicious, but then Raoul had always made good coffee. He could rustle up a meal too, having roughed it during his youth in a tough public school and later in travelling abroad.

She broke what seemed to be to her an awkward silence and addressed Sylvana.

'Thank you for a really enjoyable meal,' she said sincerely. 'I enjoyed it very much.'

Sylvana gave a pleased little smile. 'You like my cooking?' she asked, and blew smoke leisurely from her cigarette. 'I am teaching Raoul Italian cooking when he has the time, but he is so much in demand in his work that we go very slow.'

Raoul turned his head in her direction to give Suzanne a view of his strong, clear-cut profile. My presence here doesn't move him in the least, she thought, and Sylvana is teaching him about Italian food. Was that all she was teaching him? a small voice inside her whispered; don't be more of a fool than you can help. The man doesn't need teaching anything else. He knows it all. It's you who have to learn.

Raoul's smile was cynical. 'In the meantime I can enjoy your culinary efforts,' he drawled. 'Mind you, I still go along with the belief that only the French know how to cook.'

Sylvana made a playful grimace at him. 'Beast!' she scoffed. 'Just for that I shall insist that you cook me one of those wonderful French dishes one of these days.'

He gave a low chuckle and his eyes gleamed devilishly. 'When that time comes, *madame*, I shall certainly rise to the occasion.'

Suzanne's heart twisted. That charm of his was lethal! He had said that she was strong, but her strength was that of a poor butterfly beating its wings against the armour of his personality. Looking at Sylvana, Suzanne sensed the attraction she had for him transforming him into something more vibrant, more irresistible. After all, Raoul was all man and Sylvana was a woman and a half in her feminine wiles. Her tormented mind could picture Sylvana running into Raoul's arms, and the mere thought of it gave her a sense of shock mingled with utter desolation. She was a stranger, watching from afar, as other people lived out their lives. Would she herself ever know the freedom of not being bound to Raoul? Could she never cut thóse invisible chains which bound her to him? There was no future happiness for her with anyone if she could not.

Raoul was glancing at his watch. 'I have to go now,' he said, and drank the rest of his coffee. Then coming forward to stub out his cigarette in a brass ashtray shaped like a dragon on the small table, he turned to Suzanne. 'Any time you are ready, Suzanne.'

Sylvana waved them off charmingly, her long expressive fingers fluttering in a feminine gesture of farewell. Suzanne could not dislike her. She did not know the woman well enough to divide the false gestures from the true. She only knew that men would not have such qualms seeing only a delightful creature who could cook and entertain them so charmingly. Raoul could be one of these, despite his experience with women. She recalled what her father had once said about him.

'Raoul is one of those handsome devils that all women fall for—but he's nobody's fool. That's why I have no qualms about you marrying him. You will have to be clever to keep him because of his enormous attraction where other women are concerned. But almost every man loves one woman more than the rest some time in his life, and I'm sure that one will be you, Suzanne.'

Suzanne closed her eyes, hearing his loved voice yet again. If there was one all-important woman in Raoul's life it certainly was not Suzanne Dawson!

'You're very quiet. Not disappointed because I did not take you to a restaurant?' Raoul asked casually.

Suzanne opened her eyes to fix them on his lean brown hands holding the car wheel. Trying to forget their gentleness and their steely strength, she said, 'My goodness, no! The meal was delicious, and Sylvana is very entertaining.'

'Yes, isn't she? Like you, she needs a husband. She is far too feminine and vulnerable to live alone.'

Suzanne's heart went tight. 'But she is divorced, isn't she?'

The elegant long shiny front of the car eased its way miraculously between a colourful mass of Chinese humanity beneath Raoul's firm guidance.

'She's divorced, but her church doesn't recognise it as such. Sylvana is deeply religious,' he explained.

'You mean she has no intention of marrying again?'

He smiled. 'I didn't say that. Being the passionate creature she is, she probably will.'

'Is her ex-husband older than her?' Suzanne had to know.

He turned a rather jaundiced look her way and tossed her a pained smile. 'You mean is there any chance of him passing away?'

'No. I was just curious.'

'I wonder why,' he murmured, but let it pass. 'To put it crudely, the man is what is known as an insurance risk. Not only is he much older than Sylvana, he has also suffered several heart attacks.'

Suzanne went silent as the car shot forward from the congested part of the city and made for the pine-covered heights.

'Aren't you going to ask me if I'm interested?'

Raoul spoke quietly beside her, but the question startled her all the same since he seemed to be reading her thoughts. The uncanny power he had shown of reading her thoughts often in the past alerted her to put her on her mettle.

'Why should I?' she cried, quickly on the defensive. 'You flatter yourself if you think that I'm interested in you or what you do. You're free to please yourself, aren't you? Or are you?'

'I thought you weren't interested,' he replied with a tantalising inflection.

Suzanne made no answer. This was the Raoul she hated, had prayed to abolish from her thoughts, from her life. But he was here, and she had not changed much. Wildly, she thought, that's the kind of girl I am. I've killed his love for

me, only to end up loving him madly myself. How am I
going to bear it? Where do I go from here? She pulled herself together.

'You began the conversation,' she reminded him. 'How
long are you staying in Hong Kong?'

'Actually I'm using it as a base for the time being. Disappointed?'

'Why should I be? It doesn't matter to me one way or
the other.'

Suzanne knew her tone was not very convincing. She
had never been good at not speaking the truth. But Raoul
must never know of her love for him.

He said, 'Tante Jeannette is not staying here per-
manently. Did you know? When Oncle Philippe comes
back from his latest mission they plan to return to Paris.'

'Tante Jeannette did say something about it. I hope I
can see him before I return to London.'

'No doubt you will. Oncle Philippe is fond of you. Well,
here we are.' He brought the car to a standstill by the gates
of the house. Then he half turned to face her. 'Any plans
for this evening?'

'I gathered that I was spending it with Tante Jeannette,'
Suzanne replied and got ready for flight. Spending the
afternoon with him would have been a strain, but to share
with him the intimacy of night skies was too much to ask.
In her haste to leave the car she fumbled with the door.
Then Raoul was out and around her side to open it for her.

He said with a mocking inflection, 'I'd like to take you
out to dine this evening. Tante Jeannette has a telephone
call from Oncle Philippe at about nine o'clock, so she won't
mind you being out. Besides, you are in a strange country
and it will do you no harm to get your bearings. I'll pick
you up at seven.'

He had returned to his car and was gone with a lazy lift
of a brown hand and a flash of white teeth before Suzanne
had recovered her breath. Furious with herself for not being
more forthright, she stalked into the house. She would

not go, of course. The cheek of it, taking it for granted that she would be delighted to go out with him!

Tante Jeannette met her as she entered the cool room. Her eyes took in the flushed cheeks and bright dark blue eyes and she smiled.

'Did you enjoy your lunch, *chérie*?' she asked. 'Come, sit down and tell me all about it. Didn't Raoul have time to come in?'

Suzanne sank down into an easy chair as the heat in her cheeks subsided. She managed a smile, wondering how much his aunt was to be trusted.

'I think he had an appointment. He's calling to take me out this evening. He didn't ask—he *told* me he was picking me up at seven. He hasn't changed much. Still as arrogant and domineering as ever!' she ended on an indignant note.

Tante Jeannette shook her head sadly. 'I would not say that Raoul has not changed—I think he has. I cannot say exactly how he has changed, but he is more withdrawn into himself. I am very fond of him. I worry about him sometimes. I want him to settle down in a good marriage. After all, when a man reaches thirty, he has done most things in life and needs to settle down.'

Suzanne looked down at the beautiful Chinese carpet. She said slowly,

'Which leaves me again asking the question of why you asked me to Hong Kong in the first place.' She moved uneasily. 'I know you haven't much time for me since ... the break up of our marriage.' Her wide-set blue eyes sought the more serious ones of her companion almost in entreaty. 'You have every right to think badly of me.'

'In view of today's standards of behaviour I have no right to think badly of you or to sit in judgment,' Jeannette said sadly. 'Things that were taken seriously in happier days don't seem to be taken seriously any more. I don't condone divorce, but the present way of life makes it inevitable in some cases, and we have to accept it. But I never associated it with Raoul.'

'I never associated it with myself. But it happened. Maybe I'm not the marrying kind—I don't know. What do you think?'

Coolly, objectively, Suzanne looked at Jeannette as she put the question. Of what use was it trying to explain that Raoul had married her as part of a business arrangement instigated by her father? And how could one explain her own late-flowering love for Raoul—her ex-husband?

Tante Jeannette's eyes softened and she smiled. 'Life has been very generous to you, *petite*. You have many delightful qualities which, I am sure, will blossom through marriage. You are still rather young for a second venture into matrimony, and I would advise you not to seek the comfort of someone's arms merely to vindicate your own feelings.' She leaned forward in her kindly protective way. 'You must come to Paris when Philippe and I return there. I will show you all the beauties through romantic eyes. Who knows, you might find happiness there?'

Suzanne smiled. 'You've still not told me why you asked me to Hong Kong.'

Jeannette shrugged. 'Maybe I wanted to see you again. They say the English have character. I might have wanted to discover yours.'

Suzanne laughed. 'In one short visit?'

Again the characteristic French shrug. 'One can discover quite a lot over tea with a person, for instance. Don't you think it is a good idea to ring for tea? You can tell me what you plan to wear this evening when you go out with Raoul.'

Suzanne looked startled. 'Who says I'm going with Raoul this evening? I certainly have not.'

'You will if you're sensible. Oh, come on. What girl in her right mind would refuse to be wined and dined in one of the most fabulous cities on earth where money presents no problem? Besides, it will help you both to get each other out of your systems. There is nothing like the raking of dead ashes to put the last spark out altogether.'

Suzanne quelled a shudder as something occurred to her. She asked,

'Why isn't Raoul staying here while he's in Hong Kong? You did say that the company had bought this house for the benefit of its staff, didn't you?'

Jeannette looked slightly uncomfortable. 'Raoul moved out because he had no wish to embarrass you with his presence here. He is staying at his club. There is a very good English club here in Hong Kong,' she explained.

Suzanne raised a hand to the sudden heat in her cheeks. 'Oh dear!' she cried. 'I wish you'd told me, Tante Jeannette. I feel awful turning him out.'

'You mean you would not have come had you known Raoul was here?'

Suzanne shook her head emphatically. 'No, I certainly would not,' she said with emphasis. 'I want no favours from Raoul. I don't touch his money. I'm completely independent of him.'

Jeannette said meaningfully, 'Perhaps that is how Raoul wants to keep it, too. Maybe he is also doing himself a favour by not being under the same roof as you.'

Suzanne's face was the colour of a red rose as she stared at her companion with total disbelief. 'Surely you don't mean?' She began to laugh. 'It's too funny for words,' she went on. 'Do you mean to say that Raoul doesn't trust me, that he thinks I might try to make him patch things up between us if we become too friendly again?'

Jeannette was saved an answer by Sun Yu-Ren coming in with tea.

Suzanne was shattered. This was dreadful! It had never occurred to her that Raoul would regard her visit to Hong Kong as an effort at reconciliation on her part. She quivered at the injustice of it. Being a well-balanced person she had never bothered about what other people thought of her. Now she was recalling those moments in the car with Raoul when he had said that she, like Sylvana, needed a husband, that she was not a loner. He had also asked her for her reason for coming to Hong Kong in the way of sounding her out. If there was the slightest possibility that he was thinking along these lines then it was up to her to put him right. She would have to keep her date with him that evening. But she would not only make it a memorable one for him, she would make sure that it was her last.

CHAPTER FOUR

LOOKING back, Suzanne was to recall that evening with Raoul with incredulity. Preparing for the event, she had been completely undisturbed at the thought of meeting him again—oblivious of any danger in being at the mercy of his charm—just thoroughly mad. While she dressed she felt more and more pleased with herself, positively chuckling at the role she was going to play. Who does he think he is? she thought. I'll show him!

The situation called for a special dress—the colour of smooth cream with the wide sleeves and hem of the swirling skirt edged with deep bands of gold beads and diamanté. The low square neckline would be set off by a gold necklace and matching earrings. Raoul had said that she was too thin—all the better for her role as a femme fatale!

With grim determination Suzanne pinned her golden locks on the top of her small head and fastened them in place with a gold comb. Then she flicked silky tendrils of hair to curl tantalisingly by her small, neat ears. The colour of her blue eyes was deepened by adding a whisper of blue eye-shadow around them, and her mouth, which Raoul had always found so irresistible, was outlined with a seductive shade of lipstick accentuating this and the piquancy of her face.

She had trod into high-heeled golden sandals and a little honey-gold nylon fur cape was fitted snugly around her shoulders when she heard Raoul arrive.

'Have a nice time,' said Tante Jeannette, seeing her as far as the door. Then she watched Raoul open the car door for Suzanne with mixed feelings. What an enchanting creature she was, her thoughts ran darkly, with that rare quality which constitutes an exciting blend of extreme youth combined with elegance.

Raoul, handsome and very dear, with the immaculate white jacket of his evening suit enhancing the width of his shoulders, lifted a lazy hand to her as he walked around the car to the driving seat. As she returned his salute, Jeannette questioned her own wisdom in inviting Suzanne to Hong Kong. Had she been wrong to do so? Only time would tell, she thought ruefully, and went indoors.

Raoul had greeted Suzanne with slightly raised brows, murmured a greeting and had otherwise been non-committal. He did not, however, hide his surprise that she had been ready on time.

This added fuel to her anger. It brought back memories when, during their marriage, she had dawdled deliberately over dressing for important dinner dates just for the pleasure of ruffling his deadly calm. She had not succeeded, because he had called her bluff by deliberately misleading her about the time they were expected to arrive at these functions.

Raoul drove swiftly and expertly through the now thinning traffic while Suzanne fixed her eyes on the road ahead. She slackened the little evening cape, and the clever cleavage of her faultless evening dress revealed soft contours of creamy perfection.

Is this what he expects? she thought savagely. Dully she dwelt upon the fact of how strange and inexplicable pride was. Even though I'm out to seduce him up to a point, I'll freeze colder than an east wind if he so much as touches me in this instant, she thought. She felt sick at heart, but stubbornness strengthened by the hurt to her pride squared her slim shoulders.

'Where are we going?' she asked as he made for the docks.

'We're dining on one of the floating restaurants. I'm going to park the car in a warehouse near the docks, then we shall go on board a motorboat called the *Mystic Dragon* for an hour-long sail to our destination,' he informed her.

The *Mystic Dragon* was a gaily painted motor junk, and

Raoul helped Suzanne aboard with a firm hand. The light of the summer day was waning in a softly diffused kind of way, and Suzanne, held close to Raoul's strong, powerful body, boarded the boat in a dream. It was a dream she was reluctant to relinquish. But she had to play her part. She gave him a brilliant smile as they sat down, but Raoul was not looking. His face, etched against the background of sailing craft, was the face of a man withdrawn as he watched other people board the boat.

When at last the boat began to move, he whispered, 'Comfortable? It usually takes all of fifty-five minutes to reach the floating restaurant. At least there is plenty to look at on the way.'

But the scenery had faded into the background as Raoul placed a slack protective arm at the back of her seat. It struck her then in full force how utterly to the exclusion of all else he was continuing to absorb her. The knowledge was frightening. Then she hardened, recalling her mission of that evening. She would be sinuous, beguiling, swaying like a leaf in the wind towards him. How dared he think that she had come out to Hong Kong in order to make it up with him!

She looked down at the creamy wake of water tailing a hydrofoil as it left the harbour for the open sea. There was a sense of timelessness about the craft-infested waters which seemed to put one on a more even keel. If it had not been for Raoul's presence on the island she would have felt it as a kind of refuge in which she would have had the time to sort out her life. The sudden revelation of meeting him again had been startling in its reality. Here, with the cool of the water to give her a sense of calm, she was terribly aware of his nearness, and of the overwhelming attraction he held for her. His presence was warm and vibrant, sending waves not unlike electric prickings on her skin.

Rather worriedly, Suzanne wondered what effect he could have on her against her will. Were his manly charms the kind that attracted other women in the same way?

Without looking at his superb indolent grace as he relaxed beside her, she told herself that it was no business of hers if he kept a harem. He was not for her; nor she for him.

But tonight was theirs. The long evening ahead held very little pleasure for her and quite a lot of pain. That was what she was prepared to settle for. It was up to her. Her heart cried, 'Tonight is mine,' but her common sense said something far different.

The *Mystic Dragon* had edged its way alongside the floating restaurant. There was a sudden move by the people in the boat and Suzanne felt Raoul's protective arm around her as she rose to her feet, and withdrew inwardly from his contact. In that moment it seemed that they had come a long way together to a strange world utterly remote from the one they knew. It was a world of fantasy—a world in which, Suzanne told herself sensibly, she could easily lose her head.

But she had no intention of doing so. By the time they were seated at the table on the floating restaurant it was surprising how coolly she raised her eyes to Raoul's dark face to consult him over the menu. Her smile was impish as the waiter handed them small perfumed towels with which to refresh themselves while waiting for their order to be carried out.

'I'm surprised at you, Raoul,' she said lightly. 'Why not a French restaurant, since you're so convinced that French cooking is the tops?'

For one breathtaking minute in which she played a part, their eyes met and held.

He said coolly, 'You've changed.'

'Really?' with admirable calm.

He put on his tantalising drawl. 'You've calmed down. Not so restless, and you've become a beautiful woman.'

'Thanks.'

'Don't you like Chinese food?' he asked.

'I haven't tried it much yet.'

'Then prepare to enjoy yourself.'

Suzanne relaxed inwardly after eating the delicious sweet corn. Over the egg and crab soup, she relaxed outwardly and by the time they were enjoying the diced chicken with walnuts her laughter was rippling at Raoul's absurd stories heard at his club. She loved the prawns cooked in light butter balls, the pork in a velvety sauce followed by salad and an enormous bowl of fruit. The fragrant, milkless tea served during the meal in little porcelain bowls was delightful, and Suzanne sat back in her chair replete with what she regarded as manna from heaven. Raoul could have had something to do with her happy blissful state, and it was giving her the incentive to carry on with her little plan.

'What price French food now?' she challenged.

She eyed him provocatively over the rim of her little bowl of tea and waited for his answer. She knew that in his opinion she was behaving outrageously, but she forced herself to go on, ignoring the puzzled look that gleamed on occasions in his dark eyes. Had he really deluded himself into thinking that she would ask him to give her another chance? Did he dare to imagine for one moment that she had missed him at all?

She deliberately leaned against him as they boarded the *Mystic Dragon* for their return trip to the shore. Her silky head was leaning against his shoulder. She had been deliberately provocative and Raoul had played along with her, punctuating her ripples of laughter with gleams of devilment in his eyes. She wanted that sea trip to last for ever as cooler air fanned on her cheeks as the scene changed from a summer day into night. Hong Kong waited to greet them, a seductive, bejewelled haven glittering across the water in millions of lights. The rising moon was pale in comparison, and Suzanne felt her heart plunge in Raoul's arms.

She felt like a puppet, because all free will was gone. Raoul's dark head was agonisingly near and every nerve in her body screamed to life. The short stroll from the boat to where he had parked the car was taken in silence. Then he was driving away from the seedy warehouses and the harbour to go full out for the city.

Suzanne closed her eyes as the evening drew nearer to its climax. If Raoul did not ask her the reason for her strange behaviour in the next five minutes, she knew he would have put the worst possible construction on it. That being so, he would play her at her own game. Moisture oozed in the palms of her hands at the thought of it. She just had to have the strength of will to rebuke him.

Her fears grew as they scaled the heights of the island and passed the road leading to Tante Jeannette. At last Raoul stopped the car on a headland with all the panoramic view of thousands of lights twinkling beneath the stars.

'Heavenly view,' he murmured, half turning in his seat towards her. 'A night for lovers, wouldn't you say?'

Suzanne clenched her hands tightly in her lap. Steady, my girl, she reassured herself. To battle stations! His arm stole around her slender waist and he had all but drawn her into his arms when she repulsed him.

'No! No! Don't touch me—I can't bear it,' she cried, and tried to subdue her agitation. 'How dare you?'

'How dare I what?' he questioned cynically.

She wriggled in his arms, hoping to dislodge them, and failed.

'How dare you think I came to Hong Kong for a reconciliation?' she cried.

Raoul did not move. His face was in the shadow, but there was a tenseness about him that was not reassuring.

'Did I think that?'

'Of course you did!' she flared. 'Why else did you move out of the house because you knew I was coming?'

'My dear girl, I am answerable to no one for my movements, and certainly not to you. If that is what you believe and if it is the reason why you've been playing a game with me this evening, suppose we hear the rest.'

She said in dull tones, 'There's nothing to tell except that I've behaved exactly how you expected me to.'

He laughed, but there was no mirth in the dark eyes that burned with the old mockery. 'And how did I expect you to behave?'

'You know what I mean. You expected me to—to get around you and coax you into making up our differences.'

His eyes dwelt upon her, alert, speculative, and curious. 'So we can remarry?' he murmured. 'Really, *ma chère*, you are the most remarkable girl, and with the most remarkable imagination.'

'That makes two of us,' she stormed. 'How dare you jump to such absurd conclusions! I would never have come to Hong Kong if I'd known that you would be here. I—I came to be away from you, away from London and my home to think things out.'

He said quietly, 'I can well believe that. Having lost a doting father you would probably be on the lookout for someone to take his place.'

The sound of her hand coming violently into contact with his cheek was like a pistol shot on the clear night air. She drew back as from an open furnace as the heat of anger quivered in his dark face. Thoroughly frightened, she fought to free his arms, and wrenched furiously at the car door behind her. In another second she would have opened it, but Raoul had already acted. He hauled her into his arms in a flash despite her frenzied struggles to free herself. He said nothing as he relentlessly broke down her resistance, holding her closer and closer until she collapsed panting with exhaustion against him.

'That's better, *chérie*,' he commented in dangerously low tones. 'I have no idea how promiscuous you have become since we lost touch with each other, but I'm going to show you what you can expect when you try it on with a man like me.'

And he did just that. Forcing up her face, he gave her hard punishing kisses which seemed to draw out her very soul. Suzanne tried to hold on to sanity and sane reasoning as his hold threatened to crack every bone in her body.

But she could only hold on to him as his cruel mouth sought the creamy softness of her throat. When at last he thrust her from him words shot from her on each regained breath, electrified by the wild force of her passion.

'I don't want you! It was an act I put on tonight, that's all—in case you should ever think I had ever—cared for you—wanted you back. We never really—cared for each other. I wasn't your kind—you weren't mine. You never loved me, and I—treated you badly. Now I'm thankful to the roots that we're free of each other. So get it out of your head that I shall ever want you back!'

Raoul gazed down on her for a long moment. His dark eyes looked black in the half light.

'That's straight enough, anyway,' he concluded, and she heard the irony of his voice. 'Don't fret yourself that I shall ever come after you. You are fairly easy to read, and I have an excellent memory. I also have an agile brain, so don't try any tricks on me again. They could rebound on you in a way you won't like.'

He turned the car around on his last words and they shot through the night like a rocket. Suzanne felt bruised, battered and numb. Her lips were burning from his kisses and her body felt one big ache. It did not help to realise that she still did not know whether he had misconstrued her visit to Hong Kong or not. Not that it mattered. He had made it clear about his own feelings towards her. He just did not want to know.

Where did one go from here? she asked herself desperately. Would it be better for her to go back and pack as soon as she could? Fortunately, the journey back to the house was a short one and left little time for conversation. Raoul drew up at the door of the house and before Suzanne could fumble with the catch he was around the other side to help her out. To her surprise he went indoors with her.

Sun Yu-Ren admitted them, saying that his aunt had a visitor. Then Jeannette was suddenly in the doorway of the room.

'You're back early,' she exclaimed. 'Sylvana is here, Raoul. She wants your advice on some shares she holds.'

She shared her smile between the two of them, lingering for a moment on Suzanne's flushed face and then Raoul's set one.

Suzanne forced an air of calm. 'I think I'll go to bed, Tante Jeannette,' she said. 'I'm a little tired.'

Jeannette's smooth forehead puckered a little with anxiety. 'Not ill, are you, *petite*?'

'Of course not.' Her pale smile included Raoul. 'Thanks for an exciting evening. I found it most enlightening.'

CHAPTER FIVE

THE same thought that had nagged her to sleep awakened Suzanne the following morning. Should she make some excuse to Tante Jeannette and leave Hong Kong? Futile to wish that Raoul had stayed away from her for a day or so to give her time to become used to the idea of his presence, because it would not have made the slightest bit of difference. The touch of his lips where he had bruised hers in sudden anger was with her still. The kisses she had given him in the past had meant nothing. She knew that now, and the thought of him was like an ache inside her.

Unable to rest, she went early to breakfast. But Tante Jeannette had forestalled her and was already seated at the breakfast table pouring out the fragrant thin tea into delicate cups.

'Good morning, *ma chère*. Did you sleep well?' she asked kindly, passing her tea.

'Surprisingly so after the big meal I had.' Suzanne accepted her tea politely and felt forced to add, 'I hope you didn't mind me going straight to bed.'

'Not at all. You looked tired last night. You young things will insist on burning the candle at both ends.'

Suzanne sipped her tea and said tolerantly, 'Now don't you tell me I'm too thin. Someone has already told me that since I arrived.'

Jeannette's finely pencilled eyebrows rose sharply. 'Raoul?' she asked.

Suzanne felt her cheeks go hot and nodded. For a long moment Jeannette sought for something in the wide blue eyes that met hers. Then failing to find what she sought, she comforted herself with the thought that whatever Suzanne was she was never devious. Her eyes were as always as frank as a child's, which was one of those things which made her so likeable.

'Flowers for Missy. Messenger say card inside.'

Sun Yu-Ren joined them silently bearing a bouquet of dark red rosebuds with the dew still on them which he presented to Suzanne. His wide beaming smile that made his bright black eyes disappear in his yellow face evoked an answering smile from her. The room assumed a listening quality as she picked out the card tucked in the red satin ribbon beneath the cellophane wrapping. Then the four words in a masculine scrawl only too familiar leapt up at her.

'Enjoy your visit. Raoul.'

Calmly Suzanne placed the card face downwards by her plate, and asked Sun Yu-Ren to put the flowers in water. Then she lifted her eyes to Jeannette's questioning gaze.

'Raoul,' she said, aware of her burning cheeks and hoping that her companion would not notice her quivering reaction to the gift.

Jeannette had noticed and she found herself wishing that the girl would confide in her. Surely she could not be in love with Raoul after her part in their final break-up? It did not make sense. Raoul had not said anything about his marriage to her. But Jeannette knew what kind of a man he was and she would put the blame for the divorce on Suzanne every time. So she could not be blamed for saying with a sense of relish,

'A farewell gift, I suppose.'

'A—farewell gift?' Suzanne echoed with the feeling that she was sitting in the full blast of an east wind. 'You mean Raoul has gone away?'

'Yes. Did he not tell you?'

An odd tremor went through her. Something had gone out of the beauty of the day like a cloud blotting out the sun. Not long ago she had been telling herself that his absence could help her considerably in pulling herself together. Now her heart was saying something entirely different.

They ate in companionable silence while Tante Jeannette went through the post Sun Yu-Ren had brought in. Suzanne longed to ask where Raoul had gone, but fought the impulse down. She had no right to ask about him, or to tell Tante Jeannette of her deep feelings for him. What would her attitude be? she wondered. Dismay? Concern? Almost certainly not approval.

She said, 'He probably didn't think I would be interested in his comings and goings.'

'And are you?' Jeannette looked up from a letter she was tucking back into the envelope as though mildly interested.

Suzanne's colour rose under the steady regard, but she did not avoid it.

'A little,' she admitted, trying not to flinch at the understatement. 'Just because one is divorced it doesn't mean that the ex-partner ceases to exist as a person.'

Jeannette agreed. There was something about her companion that appealed very deeply, something she sensed rather than saw.

She said slowly, 'Raoul is like Philippe. One has no idea where they will land up next. I always think their secretaries know more of their movements than their nearest and dearest. Thank heaven Philippe is going to give most of his interests in the firm to someone else soon. I can hardly wait to be a real wife again instead of a constant grass widow.'

'But won't that put more work on Raoul?'

'Raoul is indefatigable; he will take it all in his stride. However, I am hoping that when he finally sees us in our wedded bliss living happily together he will follow Philippe's example and take a wife.'

'Did you know that Sylvana is teaching him Italian cooking?'

Jeannette smiled. 'Sylvana has been trying to convert Raoul into the Italian way of life from the day she met him a year or so ago. I introduced them. Sylvana had come to Hong Kong as a means of recuperating from the break-up of her marriage. I was missing Philippe dreadfully, so we became firm friends.'

Suzanne silenced a pang of jealousy. 'Then it would be ideal for her to marry Raoul in your view?'

'I don't think Raoul's next wife will be Italian. I rather think she might be French. Raoul is French—English, in that order. He still has his chateau on the outskirts of Paris and I hope he will go back to entertaining there when Philippe and I return.'

'That will be nice for you. And now if you have already made plans for today, Tante Jeannette, please don't worry about me. I would love to do some windowgazing this morning.'

Suzanne felt the need to get away from her companion just then. Strange that she had come to Hong Kong feeling desperately in need of someone who belonged even in a distant kind of way through marriage. Now she could not wait to get away. Tante Jeannette had brought the fact home to her that she was no longer one of the family. For longer than she cared to remember the thought of Raoul had obsessed her. Now she was beginning to see that he was just an emotional part of her past life. For that, she told herself, was all he was; she realised it now.

The knowledge of it was shattering—and perhaps I deserve it, she thought. I had to come all these miles to discover the truth. Far better to realise it before I end up growing frustrated, bitter, living off a hopeless love like a drug.

Tante Jeannette was saying, 'As a matter of fact I have several engagements this morning, not the least important being having my hair done. I can take you into town, but I don't want you to go wandering around too much on your own. You can come home to lunch, in fact I would prefer you to do so.'

Eating lunch by herself in the silent house, much as she loved it, was something Suzanne wanted to avoid at least until she had time to regard herself as a separate being now from the de Brécourt empire.

'Thanks,' she said brightly. 'I'd like a lift into town, but

I would prefer to lunch out. It's all right with you?'

Jeannette hesitated, seemed about to object, then said, resignedly,

'As long as you don't stay out too long. Things happen quickly here and you must promise me to take care. After all, I am responsible for you and I did promise Raoul to look after you.'

Suzanne glanced at the card containing his message at the side of her plate and told herself that his concern did not mean a thing.

'I'm used to taking care of myself,' she answered in a small voice. Later, when Jeannette dropped her off at the shops, she walked for a while with a feeling of unreality. Not yet could she believe that it was really true; that fact that both Raoul and Jeannette regarded her as outside their lives. It seemed inconceivable that she had to regard them now like ships that have passed in the night, that she had no bond with them at all. Tante Jeannette had only sent for her because she was missing her husband Philippe so much and she needed companionship.

It had been Raoul's cool acceptance of her demand for a divorce that had broken the last frail link between them. There had been plenty to take her out of herself immediately after the divorce, as her social life became hectically, defiantly exciting and full. Then her father had been taken ill, an old complaint which he had ignored and kept from her. But it had been before that when she had begun to miss Raoul. Her father's illness had been a welcome backwater for her to slide into, giving her excuses for not going out with the regular gang, and they had gradually dropped her off their social list.

Gradually Suzanne lost her thoughts in the splendour of the shops. There was an air of gaiety about the hordes of people bargaining for beautiful things and she stopped on a corner to give a beggar something after noticing that he was blind. It made her think of Alan Edge, the blind young man she had met the last time she was out shopping. She

was on that occasion about to buy a present for Tante
Jeannette, but she could not remember where the shop was.
It was a narrow street off the main road somewhere and she
distinctly remembered passing a shop that specialised in
tattooing.

As Suzanne wandered on in search of the shop, she felt
conscience-stricken at having not thought of Alan. Poor
young man, losing his sight and his girl. Had he found her?
She hoped so. At lunch time she still had not found the
shop she was looking for, but she had made several purchases including a pretty neck scarf for Tante Jeannette to
go with one of her smart suits.

Later, if she found the shop, the jade bracelet and matching earrings would come in useful as a farewell present to
Tante Jeannette for all that she had done. Suzanne was
looking round for a restaurant for lunch when she heard the
tap of a stick behind her. She turned swiftly, stared for a
moment at the fair young man with hollow cheeks and
dark sunglasses, then cried out with pleasure, 'Alan! How
nice to see you again. How are you?'

Alan wrinkled a smooth brow as he traced the quality of
her voice.

'Suzanne—Miss Dawson. It is you, isn't it?'

He held out a hand and she took it, letting his thin
fingers close around hers.

'Yes. Did you find your girl-friend Jane?'

He shook his head. 'I'm still searching,' he admitted, and
withdrew his hand from her hold to reach for a handkerchief to mop his damp forehead. 'The heat is tiring and
I'm not having much luck.'

'Poor Alan! You look dead beat. What about having
lunch with me? I was just looking around for somewhere to
eat when I heard your stick. Do say you'll join me?'

He smiled. 'I wouldn't dream of refusing. I've been thinking a lot about you since we last met. You're so young and
fresh and good for my ego.'

Suzanne linked his arm and her heart contracted at its thinness.

'I'm glad,' she said with feeling. 'I hope it helped to know that you had a friend here. Where are you staying? Is it a nice place?'

'I'm staying at the Seamen's Mission. Not bad.'

Alan sank down in his seat at the restaurant with a deep sigh of relief. He had certainly had it rough, Suzanne thought compassionately, as he told her during the meal how he had been brought up by a grandmother after losing his parents at the age of six. Jane, the girl he was seeking, had been a lifelong friend. She had been the girl next door and when he had gone to sea she had been a dancer touring the provinces and later abroad.

'She's beautiful,' Alan said dreamily. 'Long legs, black hair and a gorgeous figure. She could have had anybody as a boy-friend, but she chose me. She came out to the Far East with a dancing troupe because she knew the ship I was on would be calling at Hong Kong and Singapore for a longish stay. After the accident I was in hospital, so I couldn't come until I was better.'

'And your eyes?' Suzanne asked gently. 'Did they hold out any hope that you would see again?'

His shrug was unhappy. 'The doctors were fairly sceptical about it. They did say that there was room for hope since I was not totally blind. I can see blurs and shapes, but that's all.'

Suzanne said encouragingly, 'Maybe your eyesight will improve as your health improves. You want feeding up.'

'I've always been thin and wiry. Nothing wrong with my health or I wouldn't have got into the Navy,' he confessed jadedly. 'Funny thing is that I'm not bothered about my eyes at the moment. It's Jane I'm bothered about. I can never ask her to share the life of a blind man.'

'Don't you think you can leave that to her? After all, if she loves you ...'

'I wouldn't marry her in any case unless my eyes were

right again. I always had such excellent eyesight too. Funny that you never prize anything until you've lost it.'

Staunchly Suzanne said, 'You haven't lost it for good yet. You don't know. Wait until you find Jane—you'll feel better then. Didn't she say when she would be in Hong Kong? Haven't you any ideas about her whereabouts?'

'No.'

'Hard luck.' Suzanne was thinking hard. 'What you need is someone to take you around Hong Kong in a car to visit night clubs and theatres where she might be staying.'

He brightened. 'That's an idea, but who ...?' he demanded, looking dejected again. 'A taxi would cost the earth.'

'You could let me hire one for you,' she suggested.

He looked startled. 'Now look here, I want no charity, especially from a girl. I'll make my own way. I'm sorry if I sound ungrateful, but it isn't that at all. A chap has his pride,' he finished grimly.

She said quietly, 'Is that what you'll say if you meet Jane and she's willing to marry you?'

'I don't know. I'm so crazy about her, I just don't know.' He raked a thin hand through his blond hair. 'I wish I knew where she was. I seem to be at a dead end.'

He looked so stricken that Suzanne felt her heart go out to him.

'Have you tried the police or the British Consul? The police are the most likely ones to know since they go about in patrol cars.'

Suzanne wanted to add that there could be real danger for a girl like Jane, especially since she was so attractive, but she did not want to alarm Alan.

'I have,' he answered. 'I haven't been here long—maybe I'm too anxious to find her.'

'Mind if I help you?'

He seemed to lose some of his gloom. 'It wouldn't be right to drag you around with me. The offer is very tempting, but aren't you visiting someone here? I can hardly see you coming to Hong Kong on your own without a motive otherwise. By the way, have you a young man or anything? I hope you don't mind my asking. I don't want to get into his bad books by commandeering your company.'

Suzanne decided to be frank. 'I'm quite a free agent at the moment. Actually I'm divorced.'

'You are?'' His fair eyebrows shot up in surprise. 'You don't sound old enough to be married and divorced. Funny, I never connected you with anything like that.'

Suzanne thrust thoughts of Raoul away. 'Well?' she asked. 'Do you want me to help you or not?'

He smiled. 'I'd love you to help me,' he replied.

After lunch, Suzanne took Alan's arm and they walked around the streets, stopping at likely places displaying news of night attractions in night clubs, theatres and restaurants where Suzanne looked in vain for Jane's name among the many star attractions put on by English promoters.

Alan had produced a photograph of his love, a striking-looking girl with glossy black hair, high cheekbones and soft brown eyes in an elfin face. Suzanne liked the look of her, deciding that she did not look the kind who would let a man down even if a recent accident had made him pretty helpless, like Alan. But despite Alan's knowledge of Hong Kong—he had been there before several times in his ship —and his knowledge also of Chinese, they got nowhere in their search.

Chinese impassively shook their heads as he asked them if they knew of Jane. They hardly looked at her photograph as they lounged about on street corners or hurried along bearing a bamboo pole weighed down with soft fruit. Alan did not look up as Suzanne did for signs. He walked straight on with all his senses on the alert and Suzanne found it quite uncanny how he always managed to pick out people who were the most likely to supply them with in-formation about Jane. But it was a fruitless search. It was hours later when Suzanne, with her dress clinging to her skin and tendrils of hair curling damply on her forehead in

the heat, suggested having tea. She was not partial to eating
much herself since she would be expected to have dinner
that evening back at the Peak. It was Alan who worried
her. He did not look at all robust and what money he had
probably did not run to the kind of meals essential for his
good health. He would probably go back to the Seamen's
Mission and retire to bed on a cup of chocolate.

As she paused to look around for a likely place for tea,
she noticed a heavy door being opened in a high wall by a
lovely Eurasian girl with shining black hair, almond-shaped
eyes and a honey-smooth skin. She was wearing a black
satin cheongsam, one of those enchanting Chinese dresses
with a side split which opened demurely. A tiny coffee-
coloured lace cap on her hair and a matching lace apron
completed the uniform of a waitress. The place was
evidently a tea-garden.

A cool enchanting place in which to sit down and take
refreshment, Suzanne decided, loving the courtyard with
its pretty pots of azaleas and dwarf plants. As she led Alan
inside the courtyard she tickled his nose with a handful
of Hong Kong dollars.

She said lightly, 'We'll have tea on one condition, that I
pay for it. I would have had tea myself anyway, so I insist
upon paying.'

But Alan would not hear of it. He was fiercely independent. 'I'll pay,' he said with dignity.

It was beautifully cool in the tea-gardens as they sat on
the terrace sheltered from the sun's glare by curly over-
hanging eaves. A long fan moved lazily above their heads
and it was pleasant to sit in the peace of the courtyard behind high walls shutting out the rest of the world.

Suzanne described the scene to Alan as minutely as she
described the lovely waitress who served them with a
friendly smile. She had watched him make a good meal and
was relieved to see that he was looking more relaxed and
less tense than when they had met earlier on. She longed to
take him back with her to dinner but decided against it in

case Tante Jeannette had other guests and had made arrangements accordingly.

While they lingered over the last cup of tea Suzanne let her eyes wander around the other tables set on the veranda. A very pretty waitress was attending to an elderly English couple at the far end of the veranda and Suzanne was admiring the back view of her shapely figure in the black silk cheongsam when the girl suddenly turned to move away from the table.

In that moment Suzanne found herself looking into the startled dark eyes of an English girl, a girl who gazed from her to Alan with a startled look of recognition. Suzanne had been taken aback and watched helplessly as the girl hastily beat a retreat into the tea-house. It was Alan's missing girl-friend, Jane.

Her first impulse was to tell him. But she did not because it was clear that Jane did not want to see him. What must she do? Murmuring something about powdering her nose, she left the table and went in search of the girl. Off the veranda there was a louvred door leading to the kitchen quarters and Suzanne lingered there, uncertain what to do when. To her relief the girl who had waited at their table came and gave her a curious look before pushing open the door.

Suzanne said, 'I would like to speak to Jane. It's important.'

The girl's lovely eyes were enigmatic, but she nodded and disappeared behind. Several minutes passed and she returned to shake her head.

'No Jane here,' she said without expression. 'Excuse me, please.'

Suzanne watched her go bearing a full tray to serve her next customer. Then she went in search of the powder room. Hastily combing her hair and touching up her make-up, she pondered on her next action. She could not possibly have been mistaken. The girl was Jane, and there was that startled expression as she had seen Alan: that was proof enough.

Hastily she took pen and paper from her handbag and wrote down her name and Tante Jeannette's address. Then she hurried out of the room in search of the waitress. Fortunately she caught the girl returning to the kitchens and thrust the written note at her.

'Please, will you give this to Jane,' she said urgently. 'I must see her. Tell her that I won't tell Alan where she is until she's seen me. I am staying at the Peak.'

'You know,' Alan remarked, as they strolled away from the tea gardens, 'I can still smell the perfume of the flowers. I know it's foolish, but it remainds me of a perfume Jane used to wear.' He laughed. 'I had a feeling that she was somewhere near.'

A lump came in Suzanne's throat and she squeezed his arm. 'Let's hope she is. What are your plans for tomorrow?'

'A friend I've made in the Mission is taking me across to Kowloon and the New Territories. There's a chance that Jane might be there.'

'So I won't see you tomorrow? In the meantime I'll do my best for you. One never knows what might turn up. I think I'd better tell you my telephone number so you can memorise it in case you want to get in touch. I can look yours up in the telephone book.'

Alan squeezed her hand gratefully as he repeated the telephone number. 'I'm very grateful to you, Suzanne,' he told her humbly. 'I was feeling pretty low when I met you this morning. Now I'm feeling much brighter, and I have you to thank for it.'

To her own surprise, Suzanne herself felt much brighter than she had done on setting out that morning. She decided to walk back to Tante Jeannette's house, even though the heat was sticky. The higher she went the cooler the breeze, and she blessed Raoul's good taste in choosing a place away from the madding crowds and the city hub.

Passing elegant skyscraper hotels accommodating tourists

from all over the world, she marvelled that the Bamboo Curtain forming the border with China was only a matter of twenty or so miles away, and that although there was a fantastic number of refugees living on the water in their frail moored craft, it was still possible to get away from the feeling of overcrowding. Silence greeted her when she arrived at the house.

CHAPTER SIX

MAYBE Suzanne had expected too much when she had taken it for granted that Jane would call to see her. She had not been too happy at letting Alan go on a wild goose chase after his girl when it was all to no avail. Upon returning to the house the previous evening she had been confident that the girl would get in touch with her quite soon with some explanation of why she did not want to see Alan. But Jane had not come.

All the next day Suzanne hung around the house, taking a book out in to the garden during the morning and writing a few letters in the afternoon. Tante Jeannette went out to dinner that evening with friends leaving Suzanne alone at her own request. She dined alone, mooched around for a time, then decided to go out to the tea-house to seek Jane out. It just might be open until the light of the summer's day faded. In any case someone would be there who might help her.

The evening air was soft and humid—quite pleasant really. As she sat in the tram bearing down on the city, Suzanne told herself that whatever had stopped Jane from seeing Alan must be put right. How to set about it was another problem. As she was a romantic her whole attitude was one of wishful thinking, a total rejection of anything unpleasant which might have happened or which could happen.

Suzanne sighed. Why did life have to go wrong so often, especially on such a lovely evening, the kind for lovers when one had to smile and go on smiling.

An elderly woman boarding the tram at one of the many stops from the Peak caught her smile and returned it graciously.

The woman took a seat across from Suzanne, who was instantly impressed by her good looks. Her neatly coiffured head of champagne-coloured hair framed a face cut on classical lines. Around retiring age, she wore a fondant pink suit, the kind of model that would have been more in place in an elegant car than a tram.

'Beautiful evening,' she commented. 'Are you on holiday?'

Suzanne nodded and smiled. 'You could say that. I'm staying on the Peak. Do you live here?'

The woman nodded. 'We came when my husband retired from the Army. I'm on my way to see him—he's very ill in hospital.' She gave a quivering smile. 'Strange, isn't it, that when you marry it never occurs to you that one day one of you will die and leave the other alone?'

Suzanne asked gently, 'Is there no hope for your husband?'

'I don't really know.' The grey eyes filled with tears. 'He's had a serious operation.'

Suzanne said brightly, 'But he can recover. After all, if your husband was a soldier then he must be a fighter. The will to live can work miracles.'

The woman brightened. 'I never thought of that. You could be right—I'm very grateful to you. Thank you, my dear, for giving me fresh hope.' She sighed sadly. 'However hard I try I can't imagine life without him.'

There was a short silence while the woman struggled to control her emotions, then she went on to say that she was very happily married. Her husband was a retired Colonel and they had a bungalow with wonderful views over Hong Kong, Kowloon and the New Territories. The woman had evidently had a very happy married life and Suzanne hoped with all her heart that her husband would get better. She waved goodbye and watched the tram trundle on its way.

Was it her fancy or were all the alien sounds around her slightly sinister because the light was drawing in? She stood for a moment uncertain of her bearings. She was approaching the tea-house from a different road and she was rather confused as to the right direction. Huge neon signs flashed high above her head and trams rattled by, disappearing into shadows that were deepening ominously, or so it seemed.

When two Spanish sailors eyed her appraisingly, their hungry look devouring her charms forced her to quicken her steps. If only she could remember exactly where the tea-house was! They had come across it accidentally in such a way that she could not remember any landmarks. It had never occurred to her that the place could be difficult to find in the dark. Upon reflection she did remember a narrow alley facing the entrance gate.

For a moment she paused before a similar one before plunging down it. The alley seemed to go on and on as the shadows deepened. Most of the doors which led from the backs of shops were closed, some padlocked. Her heart plunged when a Chinese merchant coming out of one of the doors carrying a pile of boxes eyed her curiously with black slanting eyes.

She hurried on, reprimanding herself severely for thinking that he had an evil look. At last she came out of the alley into a street of high walls. It did look a little familiar. Suzanne took heart and smiled.

She was sure that this was the right street, so when she came upon a door closely resembling the one she sought, she approached it hopefully. To her relief it was unlocked. The door opened easily and her wide blue eyes took in the hive of activity. Chinese workmen were taking packing cases indoors from the yard. It was not the tea-house. For a moment Suzanne stood there helplessly staring at the men, who gestured towards her with a hurried exchange of voluble Chinese. Slowly she backed away, then turned and ran into the roadway outside right into the path of an approaching van. It towered above her, she felt the dull thud of impact and fell down, down into blackness.

*

The next three days were something Suzanne would have preferred to forget. She had awakened in hospital with her whole body aching and her head filled with pain—slight concussion, the nurse said. Indeed she had been very lucky that all her injuries had not been serious, bruised ribs, dislocated shoulder, and other minor injuries. Luckily the van she had run into had been slowing down to a stop at the time or her injuries would have been much more serious.

Tante Jeannette came to take her home on the third day. She had been very kind and Suzanne felt conscience-stricken at causing her all this trouble. It was a relief to be back in her own pretty room, to slide between the cool sheets and close her eyes.

Her head felt like cotton wool and she had never known such a feeling of depression and hopelessness as she did on that first day back with Tante Jeannette. She was very kind and asked no questions as to what Suzanne had been doing out alone in Hong Kong at night. Suzanne felt that she would have preferred to have been scolded instead of having such extreme kindness meted out to her. She had messed things up with a vengence, coming to stay with Tante Jeannette in the first place and causing embarrassment to Raoul.

Thoughts ran riot in her head until she closed her eyes against the pain they were intensifying. Tomorrow, she told herself, I shall feel better.

The next morning it was a relief to awaken free from pain. Her head still felt a little light, but her depression had gone. Sun Yu-Ren came with a light breakfast and the doctor called soon after. He was quite pleased with her and he dispelled Tante Jeannette's worried frown by telling her that her patient was all right again but must take things easy for a while. Before leaving he impressed upon Suzanne the importance of letting him know if she had any severe headaches.

As the doctor left a visitor arrived. Sylvana came in like a vivid butterfly with a yellow skirt swirling around long slim legs supported by high-heeled sandals. The sleeveless lace top matched the lace hat on her dark hair, and she carried a flower arrangement in a turquoise bowl.

'Suzanne!' she cried, in faintly accented English. 'How happy I am to find you safe and well. Poor Jeannette and I were shattered to hear that you were in hospital. But no matter. You are out again and looking just as lovely.'

Her voice was husky and warm. She bent down and kissed Suzanne on both cheeks after giving the flowers to Tante Jeannette, who had come into the room with her. Then she sat down on the bed to smile as though her coming had made Suzanne well again.

Suzanne smiled warmly at her in return, and found herself wondering if Raoul found her so irresistible. Really, it was impossible not to be friends with her.

'I'm delighted to be back with Tante Jeannette, although I'm sorry to have caused any trouble,' she said. 'Thank you for the lovely flowers.'

Sylvana playfully lifted a finger and wagged it. 'So easy for you to lose yourself in trying to find my house. You were quite near—but next time you call to see me let me know and I will come and fetch you. How are you feeling?'

Suzanne hastily collected her thoughts. So it was understood that she had gone to visit Sylvana and lost her way. Her frank nature urged her to tell these two very nice women the truth about her visit to the tea-house. But on second thoughts it occurred to her that it would be far better to let the whole incident slide into the past. Her visit had brought enough problems. How could she add to them?

'I'm feeling fine, thanks,' she said, and her smile included Tante Jeannette, who had placed the turquoise bowl of flowers on the dressing table.

'It's very kind of you, Sylvana. You are so clever at arranging flowers,' said Tante Jeannette softly.

Sylvana laughed as she thanked Tante Jeannette. Her eyes sparkled at the praise and Suzanne admired the strong, clear-cut profile, the beauty of her hair and eyes. One could not blame Raoul for being attracted to her. Sylvana, she decided, could storm any man's heart and leave her impression there for ever. Suzanne recalled the strength of Raoul's hands closing over her own. Did she share a similar memory with Sylvana? Had she known the strength of his hands, and what was more, the steely grip of his arms around her, his demanding kisses?

Suzanne was alarmed at the way her thoughts ran. What if Sylvana and Raoul were lovers? It was no business of hers. It was a shock to discover that she was feeling possessive over her ex-husband when she had no right to do so.

Sylvana was saying, 'Thank you, Jeannette, for praising my flower arrangement. Praise of any kind makes me feel so good. I miss Raoul in that respect so much. He has this gift of making a woman feel special and rather wonderful. The days he has been away seem like a year, and he will be away at least another week or so.'

The delicate perfume Sylvana used was all around her. Suzanne wondered if that was familiar to Raoul too. She was realising that he had kept in close contact with Sylvana and given her a good idea of what he was doing and how long he would be away. Whether he had given the same information to Tante Jeannette, Suzanne was not to know. But surely it was natural enough for him to keep in touch with the woman he loved, Sylvana? Sternly, Suzanne told herself not to be so idiotic as to be upset about this too.

It was time, she realised, that all relations between Raoul and herself were at an end, finished. That went for Tante Jeannette too. Her loyalties lay with her nephew Raoul and it was not the intention of her, his ex-wife, to stretch those loyalties to include herself. This would be her last visit to Madame de Brécourt, as she would be known to Suzanne Dawson from now on.

Suzanne left her bed feeling strange and stiff. She washed and dressed lethargically for lunch with Tante Jeannette and Sylvana. She brushed the dull gold hair into a

gleaming silkness, added colour to her face by a touch of
lipstick, and was ready. Lunch was laid by the open
windows which gave a panoramic view of Hong Kong
harbour.

Sun Yu-Ren was there to tempt her into eating her lunch.
He served each course with the obsequious charm of one
happy to give her the opportunity to enjoy his culinary
skills. A delicious iced soup was followed by thin tender
slices of beef with bamboo shoots and fried rice. There was
young duckling with cherries and pineapple and a sweet
which reminded Suzanne of snowflakes, a sugary vegetable
served in almond-flavoured milk. In an all-out effort to
please him, Suzanne not only ate all her portions, she
thoroughly enjoyed them.

Later, they sat admiring the view while Sylvana lit a
cigarette and Suzanne listened to her conversation with
Tante Jeannette. She was beginning to love Hong Kong.
There was a magic about it. It was easy to imagine how the
place could take a grip on oneself, making one reluctant
to leave. Unless one was wanting something else from life.

Take Tante Jeannette, for example. She wanted Oncle
Philippe and her beloved Paris. Sylvana wanted to marry
again and hankered for Raoul. Suzanne could not say what
she herself wanted from life. All desire for any particular
thing was non-existent. It was the aftermath of the accident,
of course. Her terror of the Chinese workmen, her fleeing
from them, had been a shock in itself. And it had been so
funny, looking back on it, to be terrified of a few men
who were merely carrying out their job of unloading a van
in order to carry the goods into a shop.

The scene before her faded into the heat. Once again
she could see the ascetic features of the doctor in charge of
the unit in which she had worked for under-privileged
children. He was smiling down at her and shaking his head.

'You must go home now,' he had said. 'You have done a
wonderful job here, but you have given too much of yourself. But that is your nature. Go home and find a nice hus-

band who will take care of you. I hope you find what you have been seeking here. Now it is time to go.'

Soon it would be time to go again, away from Hong Kong. Suzanne shook herself out of her mental lethargy and decided to stop feeling sorry for herself. She was being very ungrateful not to respond to the kindness around her.

Sylvana roused her by drawing her into the conversation and things became normal as the shadows of the last few days faded. Replete with good food and good company, Suzanne felt her eyelids drooping. Her breathing became deep and even as she slept.

The deep baritone voice smote her ears like a gong, awakening her from her sleep, and she opened her eyes to discover that she had fallen asleep after lunch and that Sylvana and Tante Jeannette had left their seats beside her. Their voices were now mingling with the masculine one that had awakened her—Raoul. What was he doing here when he was not expected yet for some time?

A cold sweat oozed on her temples. She did not want to see him again, not yet. The revelation that she was no longer a part of his or Tante Jeannette's life was too new and too painful. But how could she evade them, for their voices were nearer now coming in her direction. In a panic, she rose to her feet, only half awake and a little dazed with the aftermath of the tranquillisers prescribed by the doctor. Her head spun round like a top and she had to grip the back of a chair to save herself from falling.

Then Raoul was there. For a moment he seemed lost for words as he looked down at her, his dark eyes intent. The air of aloofness which Suzanne associated with him was no longer there as he took in her pale face and air of helplessness.

'Suzanne, *ma chère*! Are you all right?' His arms were around her then supporting her and as the lightheaded feeling grew weaker, she realised that a greater pain was taking its place. His arms were around her bruised ribs, but somehow the pain did not matter because she was being held close against him.

Tante Jeannette was saying with agitation, 'I'm sure she got up too soon. Sylvana and I will help her back to bed.'

The thought of causing more trouble helped Suzanne to pull herself together more than anything else could have done.

'No, no, please! I'm quite all right.' she cried, pushing Raoul away. 'I—I was a trifle lightheaded, that's all.' She gave a small laugh. 'I don't know what got into me. I've never gone to sleep after lunch before—I do apologise.'

Raoul gazed down at the moisture on her temples where her hair clung in curly tendrils giving her a vulnerable look, and the blurred beauty of her face as she strove to hide her distress sent him into action. Lifting her in his arms, he bore her away beneath the astonished gaze of Sylvana and Jeannette.

'I'm taking her to her room,' he said over his shoulder as he strode away.

Suzanne lay against him, painfully aware of the strength and tenderness in his arms. Quite gently but with indisputable strength he laid her down on the bed. His dark eyes were grim, though he spoke in a tone all the more arresting because of its softness.

'How is the head? I believe you had a slight concussion among other injuries.' He laid the back of his fingers against her forehead. 'You said you went lightheaded. How do you feel now? I want the truth. Any pain?'

Suzanne forced herself to look up at him, at the wide shoulders, the arrogant brown face, the near-black eyes, and tried to make light of the situation by speaking firmly.

She said protestingly, 'I have no pain in my head. I'm all right, honestly I am. Anyone can—can go lightheaded, if they happen to move too quickly, and that's exactly what happened.'

He said grimly, 'Fit enough to go on a ten-mile walk?' He smiled sardonically and removed his fingers from her forehead. 'Your skin is hot. You have a slight temperature.'

Suzanne could not have agreed with him more, although she did not admit it. No wonder she had a temperature! Her heartbeats were still hammering away from the thrill of being in his arms. And they were likely to continue hammering as long as he stood there looking so lean, tanned and heartbreakingly handsome.

'I'm just warm, that's all. I feel fine.'

'Five minutes ago,' he reminded her, 'you nearly passed out.' He paused on a sigh which seemed to say that she exasperated him profoundly, and added, 'I suggest that you stay in bed for the rest of the day. I'm not sure whether you should have the doctor or not.'

He blue eyes widened in dismay. She cried, 'Oh no, not the doctor, please! I'd feel awful bringing him out on a fruitless errand. I don't know what all the fuss is about.'

'Raoul is only doing what he knows is best for you, Suzanne. We have been very worried about you.'

Tante Jeannette had entered the room with Sylvana. Her manner and tones were frigid. But before Suzanne could take in the older woman's abrupt manner, Sylvana had drifted across the room to the bed on a wave of expensive perfume to take Raoul possessively by the arm.

'You really must allow us to take care of you,' she cooed sweetly.

The remark annoyed Suzanne. She would have liked to point out that it was nothing to do with her. But the warmth of Sylvana's voice disarmed her.

She smiled. 'As it happens, Sylvana, I feel well enough to take care of myself. I had a little dizzy spell, but it's nothing to get worked up about.'

Her smile, which had included them all, was her only defence against the hurt Sylvana was inflicting by putting her outside their little circle.

'All the same, *ma chère*, I think it is wise for you to stay in bed for the rest of the day.'

There were soft undertones in Tante Jeannette's voice

brought on by the sight of Sylvana and Raoul so close together. So, Suzanne thought bitterly, no wonder she wants
me to stay in bed out of the way!

Raoul said, 'I'm going to call for the doctor. Concussion, however slight, is nothing to be taken lightly.'

He looked a little put out, and Suzanne felt a pang at the
thought that he resented her presence in Hong Kong and
the trouble she was causing.

It was Sylvana who voiced a protest. 'But surely you
heard Suzanne say that she feels all right, Raoul? Would
it not be better to wait for a while to see how she feels after
a rest in bed?'

'No, it would not. I will put in a call for him now,' he
said firmly.

Fleetingly Suzanne felt his cool fingers rest for seconds
again on her forehead, but she was too miserable to react in
any way. Then he turned abruptly and strode from the
room.

Tante Jeannette moved over to the bed and said gently,
'You must not mind Raoul's high-handedness. He feels
responsible for you because you are under his roof.' She
placed a hand over Suzanne's as it lay on the bed. 'Would
you like us to help you to undress?'

'No, Tante Jeannette, thank you,' Suzanne answered,
wishing she did not feel so choked up. 'I shall stay here
until the doctor arrives. I'm sure he'll be very surprised at
being summoned again so soon—but there it is.'

Tante Jeannette sighed and Suzanne intercepted a look
between her and Sylvana which suggested that they should
go. She watched them leave the room with a sense of relief,
but she could not relax. There was too much on her mind.
She wondered about Alan Edge and his girl-friend Jane,
and her lips twisted wryly at the thought of her own
blundering. Too late, she realised that Alan ought to have
been told that Jane was working in the tea-house. But
would it have solved anything? There was some reason
why Jane did not want to see him. If only she could have

found out the reason for Jane going into hiding! She might have been the means of bringing them together again. Yet much as she rued her accident the thought was that it could have been much worse.

Suzanne was half way between sleep and consciousness when she was aware of someone standing by her bed, and she opened her eyes to see the doctor smiling down at her.

Raoul, tall, sardonic and with graceful ease, stood at the foot of the bed. Wishing that he was a thousand miles away, Suzanne addressed the doctor.

She said apologetically, 'I'm sorry you had to come. I'm quite all right.'

He said without preliminaries, 'Tell me what happened.'

With her eyes fixed on the square capable hand on her wrist taking her pulse, she told him. His examination was brief. He asked if she had any head pains and did not appear to be a bit put out by being summoned again so soon.

All the time Raoul stood there with an air of patience and relaxation. Suzanne knew that he sensed her uneasiness in his presence and he was enjoying it. She blinked rapidly and a stubborn note crept into her voice.

'Doctor, if you're going to tell me to stay in bed for the rest of the day, you'll be the fourth person to do so,' she said ungraciously.

The doctor straightened and his twinkling eyes focused on Raoul at the foot of the bed. Suzanne summed the middle-aged doctor up as a family man who was no fool where human emotions were concerned. Her pulse was hardly likely to slow down while Raoul was there, and the doctor could be aware of this.

Smoothly he said, 'Good advice. You are fortunate to have people around you who are concerned about your welfare. Monsieur de Brécourt did the right thing to send for me when he did. Another day in bed will work wonders.'

He gave them a penetrating look from beneath bushy grey brows. If he was curious about their relationship, he did not show it. Raoul de Brécourt, he knew, was very popular with the ladies, his wife included. The girl with her golden hair strewn over her pillow like silk, and her deep blue eyes regarding him with open candour, made him very aware of his age. He found himself wishing that he was in his twenties again. Lucky Monsieur de Brécourt! An interesting couple.

Raoul said, 'Thank you for coming, doctor. Would you care for a drink before you go?'

The doctor refused politely, saying that he had to hurry away to another patient. He gave Suzanne's hand a reassuring pat and strolled with Raoul from the room. Suzanne, waiting for their voices to die away, told herself that she hated all men.

The day passed with Tante Jeannette calling in to see her from time to time. Sylvana brought her tea and tiny almond cakes during the afternoon and said that she was invited to dinner that evening. Suzanne felt a dull pain at her heart at the thought of Raoul sharing his evening with her, then she decided to be sensible about it. After all, Raoul had been dining with Sylvana long before she herself came to Hong Kong.

Early evening brought Tante Jeannette with a dozen red rosebuds arranged in a Chinese vase which she set down on the dressing table beside the bed. Suzanne recalled similar bouquets sent to her while she had been in the hospital. Raoul, she remembered with pain, had always sent her roses.

She said warmly, 'Thank you, Tante Jeannette. They're lovely.'

Tante Jeannette spent a few moments moving the stems in place, then she stood back to admire the effect.

'Yes, they are lovely, aren't they? I presume that they are your favourite flowers,' she said without rancour.

'Yes, they are, but how did you know? I wasn't aware of telling you.'

'Raoul sent them. He has sent flowers every day since

your accident, so I presumed that roses were your favourite
flowers.' Tante Jeannette's eyes were saying something else
too, thought Suzanne, and she was not too happy about it.

She spoke her thoughts aloud with a lightness she was far
from feeling.

'Red roses for love,' she scoffed. 'But don't worry—
Raoul didn't have that in mind when he sent them.'

Tante Jeannette looked uneasy. 'May I ask you something?' she said.

'Ask away.'

'What are your feelings for Raoul? I know you never
loved him—you couldn't have treated him like you did if
you had. Please forgive my impertinence in asking, but I
would like to know.'

Suzanne blessed the tide of hot colour flooding her face.
She said offhandedly, 'It all happened so very long ago, and
we're divorced. A bit too late in the day to discuss personal
feelings, don't you think?'

Tante Jeannette came across to the bed with her graceful walk and bent to straighten the coverlet.

'You're not happy, are you, Suzanne? I've watched you
since you came, and you have a haunted look about you. I
know you lost your father and that it was a big blow, but
there is something else, is there not?' Her expression was
the kind to invite confidences, but Suzanne knew she could
not confide in her much as she would like to. No one must
know of her love for Raoul. And it would probably upset
Tante Jeannette enormously.

She said sadly, 'No love affair, Tante Jeannette, if that's
what you're thinking. If it upsets you to have me here, I'll
go.'

The older woman looked shocked at the very thought of
her going.

'Oh, no! Please stay,' she cried. 'You like it here, don't
you, *petite*?'

Suzanne said gallantly, 'Who wouldn't? Hong Kong is a
wonderful place and you've been a dear for having me. I

hope you won't regret it—I know I shan't. It's helped me considerably, coming here.'

'I am very happy to hear it.' Tante Jeannette relaxed visibly and looked thoughtful. 'I forgot to tell you—someone telephoned you this morning, someone named Alan Edge. I told him to telephone you again this evening. I thought with you not being well you might feel more up to taking the call tonight. He is calling you at seven o'clock.'

Suzanne brightened visibly. 'Did he leave any message?' she asked hopefully.

'No, and I did not tell him about your accident.' A pause and Tante Jeannette added as an afterthought, 'You are not unhappy about this man, are you, *ma chère*?'

Suzanne shook her head. 'Not in the way you mean. I met him on the plane coming over. He's staying in Hong Kong.'

'I see,' said Tante Jeannette in a tone which clearly implied that she did not. She hesitated as she straightened after smoothing the coverlet on the bed. 'Sun Yu-Ren will bring you your evening meal on a tray.' Her smile was disarming. 'He has prepared something special for you. Do not let him down, will you? It is sure to be delicious. He is very fond of you—we all are.'

Suzanne wished it was true. She said tightly, 'I'll do my best. I'm very grateful—everyone has been so kind.'

When Tante Jeannette had gone she lay for a long time gazing at the flowers Raoul had sent. Red roses for love, when he had never loved her. She recalled the flowers he had sent to her at the hospital and wondered why his card had never been there. Granted, she had been too ill at the time to bother about them, but not today. Was there no card today either? A search around revealed nothing, not even when she lifted the Chinese vase of roses to look underneath. If there had been a card then Tante Jeannette had kept it.

Poor Tante Jeannette, guarding her beloved nephew from a femme fatale, one Suzanne Dawson! She could have laughed if it had not hurt so much. By the time the telephone call from Alan Edge came through she was awaiting it eagerly. Nice to have a friend, she thought, cynically.

'How are you, Suzanne?' he asked. 'I'm calling from the Seamen's Mission after another disappointing day searching. I telephoned you this morning to ask you to come with me to Kowloon, but you weren't available.'

'Sorry about that,' she answered, deciding not to burden him with the details of her accident. He had enough troubles of his own without her adding to them. It was on the tip of her tongue to tell him about seeing Jane at the tea-house, but she could not without making another attempt to find her—to discover why she was hiding. She would go in daylight next time; tomorrow, perhaps. Her resolve to go was strengthened when Alan told her that he was going again to the New Territories the following day with his friend from the Seamen's Mission. He sounded depressed and she tried to cheer him up by promising to let him know immediately she had any news of Jane. What a pity that it was not possible for him to come to the house to spend the evening with her. But Tante Jeannette would hardly approve of her entertaining him in her bedroom, and she could just imagine Raoul showing his disapproval.

Somehow the evening drifted by. Sun Yu-Ren brought her evening meal and she managed to eat enough of it to bring a smile to his face when he came later to collect the dishes. As the hours crept by her thoughts turned towards the three people dining without her. Soon Raoul would be leaving for his club. He would probably take Sylvana for a run in his car before taking her home. It was easy to imagine them together, Sylvana sitting beside him in the car with her lovely head thrown back to show her attractive profile. Her beautifully modelled hands would make expressive gestures as she talked, and Raoul would turn to look at her from time to time as he drove with a faintly cynical yet entirely affectionate interest.

Sylvana clearly was in search of a husband, and who bet-

ter than Raoul de Brécourt, who was wealthy, handsome,
exciting, and amusing? Her religion could have been used
as a cloak to hide behind in stalking a husband, a ruse
perhaps unrealised by herself; Suzanne argued that it must
be something of the sort.

Tormented by such painful thoughts as she was, it was
hardly surprising that sleep evaded her. By half past eleven
the house was silent, but Suzanne felt anything but restful.
At last she threw back the bedclothes and put on a wrap
that matched the pretty blue nightdress. The long, loose
cape sleeves had large blue flowers printed on a black background. Flimsy and subtly feminine, it swirled around her
slender figure as she tied the large bow at her throat.

Minutes later she was stealing from her room in noiseless
mules to seek fresh air on the terrace. A few deep breaths
of pure night air would help to induce sleep. The lights
were out, but moonlight filtering through the french
windows guided her to the terrace. She smiled a little as
she stepped outdoors. It was a beautiful evening.

A slight breeze was teasing the golden bells attached to
the curly corners of the eaves above her head, filling the air
with soft sweet sounds. Then her heart lifted. A tall, wide-
shouldered figure turned swiftly at the far end of the
terrace before she could draw back out of sight.

He had merged into the shadows, for the clothes he was
wearing were soft and dark in colour. As he drew nearer she
saw the silk scarf tucked at the firm brown throat. The next
moment he was confronting her and making it impossible
for her to escape without walking round him. The silence
crackled with electric waves as Suzanne held her breath.

'Ah, a beautiful ghost,' he said sardonically, 'and it is not
yet the witching hour of midnight.'

His eyes narrowed down on the gleaming hair silvered by
moonlight, the deep blue of her widely-spaced eyes, before lingering on the flimsy attire that revealed the seductive youthful curves of her slender figure. Lazily, he reached
out a brown hand to lift a lock of her hair in careless

fingers. His eyes strayed over the creamy softness of her neck.

Suzanne continued to stare at him in wide-eyed disbelief. Raoul here, in a dressing gown, could only mean one thing. He was now staying in the house. With heartbeats that threatened to choke her she pulled herself together.

She said, 'I thought you were staying at your club.'

'I was, but I am here now. Do you mind?' sardonically.

'What happened? Did they kick you out?'

He laughed softly and his teeth showed up very white against the dark tan of his face. 'No. Surprised?' he asked, and wound her hair slowly around his finger.

'Why should I be? You always do as you please—that's nothing new,' she cried indignantly.

'No?' he mocked. 'What is new—a very pretty blonde by the name of Suzanne Dawson?'

Was he laughing at her? Suzanne stepped back and the silken coil of her hair slipped through his fingers. Uneasily, she was aware of every nerve in her body tingling at his nearness. The night assumed a magic quality around her and she closed her eyes, finding that speech was beyond her.

'Sit down,' said Raoul. 'How are you feeling?'

He drew a chair forward and she sat down while he leaned back carelessly against the window frame of the open door. Surreptitiously she looked up at his clear-cut profile and her heart bled. It was so strange to find him here in the house when she had been picturing him with Sylvana.

'I'm feeling fine,' she answered. 'Where is Sylvana? I thought she was here to dinner this evening.'

'She came. Now she is at home.' He paused, then, 'Who was the man who telephoned you this evening?'

He turned to look down at her and she stared back at him for long seconds with a frown. Then her brow cleared. She said lightly,

'Someone I met on the plane coming over. Why?'

He shrugged, a typical French gesture which added to his charm. She saw the hand slipped casually into his pocket, the strength of his wide shoulders, the thick dark hair curling in crisp tendrils in his neck, and she ached for him.

He said crisply, 'This is not London. Hong Kong is not a good place for a young and attractive woman to be alone in. Do you know this man? Has he connections here?'

Her blue eyes held sparks. 'You have no right to ask questions concerning friends of mine. What I do, where I go, and with whom, is none of your business,' she challenged.

He considered this, said unperturbedly, 'Hong Kong is hardly the best place for an attractive young woman to make casual friendships. While you are under my roof I am responsible for you.'

'When I was invited here I didn't expect a jailer!'

His mouth thinned. 'Don't be so naïve,' he said tightly. 'It is for your own good. In future you will bring any friend you make here to the house. Understand? You need protecting against yourself.'

Suzanne spread her hands on the arms of her chair and gripped hard. How dared he give her orders? His eyes glittered and his teeth were closed tight with distaste and irritation, but she did not care.

'Why should you be so concerned?' she cried. 'I don't even bear your name. You look after your own life and leave me to look after mine!'

'Maybe I feel I owe it to your father to look after you.' Suddenly he was bending over her with his hands covering hers on the arms of the chair, making her virtually a prisoner. 'Besides,' a sardonic smile lifted the mobile corners of his mouth, 'remember that talk we had earlier on when you said that you regarded the invitation here as an offer of a sanctuary. I said then that I was going to see that you returned to London in one piece, and I intend to keep that promise.'

Her heart began to thump as vitality seeped into her from

the warmth of the hands covering her own. Raoul was like a dynamo re-charging everything he happened to come into contact with. It was shattering to know that he could affect her emotions in this way. Her resistance was weakening, and a feeling of dismay swept over her lest he should discover that his power over her stemmed from her hopeless love for him. Perhaps something in her wide blue eyes got through to him, for his manner changed.

His voice grew gentle. 'Do not look so shattered, *ma chère*,' he murmured with a hint of a smile. 'You will be grateful to me in the end.'

Suzanne drew back in her chair, finding his nearness suffocating, and she struggled to free her hands. He released them, straightened his tall frame and pushing his hands inside the belt of his robe, waited for her to speak.

Now that he was no longer close to her Suzanne assumed a degree of calm. 'Thank you. I suppose I ought to feel highly honoured that you're prepared to squeeze me in between your many commitments.'

He smiled. 'I said something just now that I feel I must qualify. I implied that I was free to do as I wished, but that is only partly true. It is only in the past two years that I have begun to realise how much a prisoner I have been to my work. All the dedication has denied me the right to live my life as I want it, in short, to follow my own pursuits. Now I have my priorities right I intend to change all that. I intend to go for all the worthwhile things in life. No need to tell you what they are—you would not be interested.'

She wanted to cry out, But I am! but her lips were sealed. She swallowed on a lump in her throat and tried to keep her tones light.

'It—it wouldn't have anything to do with Oncle Philippe's decision to retire, would it? I know Tante Jeannette wants him to retire very much. She's been very lonely without him.'

'We have been discussing it for some time. I think we have things how we want them now.'

'You mean you're both going to retire?'

'Not exactly. We shall keep our hand in but concentrate more on a home base. There is no one to carry on the family name at present, and I want to remedy that.'

'You ... you mean raise a family?' Suzanne could not meet his eyes as she asked the question. She could not bear to think of him and Sylvana.

'Of course. What are your plans for the future?'

'I'm learning to live from day to day,' she answered primly.

He laughed. 'That is the kind of answer I would have expected from a very old lady. Have you considered marrying again?'

With unnatural calm, she said, 'No.' Further words failed her, but he waited, standing above her until she was forced to add, 'It isn't a subject I care to discuss.'

'You mean not with me? Does it by any chance have anything to do with the man you met on the plane?'

A sense of anti-climax was creeping over her. His nearness, the intimate conversation, the feeling that they were now as close as they ever would be acted like a battering ram against her defences. Soon she would be giving herself away hopelessly and irrevocably.

Suppressing her agitation, she excused herself by pleading tiredness.

His dark eyes probed her pale face as she rose to her feet and he asked sharply, 'Are you all right? No head pains?'

Again those long fingers were testing the heat of her forehead, and she drew back as if his touch stung. She wanted to request him to let her pass, but she dared not trust her voice. She could only stand with her face averted.

Raoul bent his head to look at her. 'Are you all right?' he repeated reaching out for her hand. 'Your hand is cold. You are going to catch a chill,' he added roughly.

If she had been cold before now the light firm touch of his hand sent a sudden warmth through her body setting an inner desire alight.

'Stop it!' she cried. 'I'm not an idiot! I'm all right.'

Looking blindly up at him, she knew that it was imperative for her to get away from him quickly before she lost control altogether. Another moment and she would be collapsing in his arms with her face buried in his chest. Fear sent her voice higher than she intended.

'Will you please leave me alone? I hate you to touch me!'

He released her hand at once and she fled. Once in her room she leaned back against the closed door still quivering at her narrow escape from utter humiliation. So he was going to marry Sylvana and raise a family. A sharp agonising sense of loss for all that she might have had brought the tears. They spilled over. Life was going to be very empty indeed without him.

CHAPTER SEVEN

As it happened Suzanne did not have to go in search of
Jane at the tea-house. Sun Yu-Ren arrived with her breakfast just as she was on the point of getting up, and she
accepted it gratefully. She had been dreading meeting
Raoul at the breakfast table.

'Missy eat up all breakfast, plees,' Sun Yu-Ren pleaded
with his wide smile. 'Tea plenty hot. All favourite things
like melon.'

Suzanne lingered over the meal, eating more than she
would have done in order to kill time and also to please
Sun Yu-Ren. Later, washed and dressed, she inspected her
face in the dressing table mirror and saw that the colour
was back in her cheeks, her eyes were clear with only a
shadow of the agony she had gone through the previous
night. The pale blue silk suit looked cool and chic, the
high-heeled sandals showed the long slim gracefulness of
her pretty legs, but Suzanne could not have cared less.

The morning was golden and warm, giving her a sense
of wellbeing as she checked the contents of her handbag to
make sure that the map of Hong Kong was there in case
she lost her bearings again. Sun Yu-Ren's anxious perusal
of the tray she carried to the kitchen warmed her heart and
his satisfied smile when he saw that she had made a good
breakfast lighted up the kitchen.

The house was quiet and peaceful, with only the thought
of Raoul to agitate the calm. His deep voice seemed to hit
her ears like a gong as it came in all its musical cadence on
the clear morning air. She paused with a hand to her throat.
The next moment she walked on to the terrace with nerves
tense and came upon him leaning nonchalantly against the
frame of the terrace window gazing down at an elfin girl

with the small body and long legs of a dancer. The smooth dark curtains of hair framing a small piquant face gave her an attractive, almost Oriental look as she shone up at Raoul with laughter in her dark eyes. Like Raoul, she was smoking a cigarette, and her face registered instantly. Jane! Alan's Jane, Suzanne thought with a sense of shock.

Raoul looked darker and more vital than ever in light slacks, a silk lightweight shirt and a cream paisley scarf tucked at his firm throat. He was enormously attractive in the clear morning light, and Jane evidently thought so too, for she was gazing up at him entranced.

Without looking at him Suzanne knew that the glint of mocking humour in his eyes would disappear when he saw her. She told herself emphatically that she did not care. Her emotions were well battened down now that she knew that Suzanne Dawson meant no more to him than this very attractive girl gazing up at him so intently.

Raoul said without preliminaries, 'A visitor for you—Miss Jane Owen. I will leave you together.'

'Good morning,' said Suzanne, and dropped into a chair opposite to her visitor and waited.

'You're wondering, aren't you, what on earth I'm doing here?' Jane smiled and looked apologetic at the same time. 'I hope you'll forgive the intrusion and the early hour, but I had to see you.'

Suzanne said composedly, 'I'm glad you've come. I went to try and see you at the tea-house again and lost my way.'

Jane looked sheepish. 'I'm sorry—but you see I had no idea of your connection with Alan.'

As she leaned forward to tap ash from her cigarette on to the ash tray on a nearby table, Suzanne noticed the expensive gold bracelet on her arm. Like the exquisite wristwatch she consulted, it was not the kind of jewellery one would expect a dancer to have. Nor was the expensive perfume.

Intrigued in spite of herself, Suzanne asked, 'What made you decide to come to see me?'

The girl shrugged. 'I thought it over after following you and Alan when you left the tea-house that day. I almost made myself known to you both then. It's been a very hard decision to make. I intended to come and see you several times, but always my nerve failed me. You see, I had no idea how far I can trust you.'

Suzanne smiled. 'You don't now, but you can.'

Jane gave a sigh of relief. 'Thank you. I was hoping I could—you looked kind of sweet and understanding. I don't know how much Alan has told you about us, but I came to Hong Kong with a dance company intending to see him. I suppose you know we missed each other?'

Suzanne nodded.

'Everything began to happen. The company folded up when we were in Singapore and we were stranded. Fortunately my friend Carol met and got married to a wealthy Eurasian while we were there and I stayed at their house while they were away on honeymoon. While I was there I learned to love the luxurious way of life and the comfort. This bracelet is a birthday gift from Carol. The wristwatch was given to me when I was chief bridesmaid at her wedding. Carol gave me some of her clothes before I left to take a job at the tea-house where you saw me. I'm very grateful to you for not giving me away to Alan,' she added. 'I wanted time to think.'

Suzanne digested this, then said dryly, 'There's no problem as I see it. Either you love Alan enough to marry him or you don't.'

Jane crushed out her cigarette into an ash tray. She raised dark eyes clouded by indecision.

She said slowly, 'Going by the way you dress and talk I would say that you've never known what it's like to be poor, really poor. Well, I have, and believe me, it's no laughing matter, especially in my job as a dancer. I've been in some pretty crummy digs. I've seen how the wealthy enjoy life, but I can't deny that I might have settled for Alan. However, things are different now. Together we could have made a good life for ourselves, but now I ask myself what prospects are there for us.'

'But Alan might get his sight back. There's always that chance,' Suzanne insisted. 'Would you marry him if he regained his sight?'

'I don't know. I honestly don't know.' Jane covered her face with shaking hands, and Suzanne gazed down helplessly at the glossy black head. Was she doing Alan a good turn by acting as Cupid, or was he better off without her? Was Jane as mercenary as she appeared to be? Alan would be better off without her if she was. Suzanne teetered, then plunged.

'Tell me,' she demanded, 'did your friend marry for money?'

It was obvious that Jane was shocked by the question.

'Goodness, no!' she cried, looking up in horror at the suggestion. 'Carol's husband is a beautiful man. She fell head over ears in love with him and he with her. He's a good looking man with that innate charm and magnetic personality that most women go for. The man who's just left us has the same physical attraction. Is he French?'

Suzanne smiled. 'Raoul? Almost.'

Jane laughed. 'He's very good-looking. I could go for him in a big way, and I don't even know his name. He happened to see me arrive here and asked me who I wanted to see. I said the lovely blonde. Are you French? He called you Suzanne.'

She shook her head. 'The name Suzanne was pure coincidence. Father wanted me named Susan, but Mother preferred Suzanne.'

'What's your other name?'

'Dawson. Suzanne Dawson.'

'And the man Raoul?'

'Raoul de Brécourt.'

Jane was impressed. 'Is he married?'

'No.'

Jane looked more impressed. 'I bet he's wealthy—he

has that air that shrieks of money. I don't mean to be vulgar, but I must admit I'm curious. Are you and he engaged?'

'No, nor likely to be. I'm here at the invitation of his aunt.'

Jane sighed. 'Lucky you! You'd be a fool not to grab him.'

Suzanne laughed. 'You haven't asked how I met Alan. I met him on the plane coming to Hong Kong. Then I saw him again in town later. I think he's a very fine young man. He's very brave to come out here, handicapped as he is by not being able to see to search for you. He's very worried about you. He loves you very much and he's going to be very hurt when you tell him the truth.'

Jane looked dismayed. 'But I don't have to tell him.'

'Of course you will,' Suzanne said sternly. 'He's searching for you. He's gone to the New Territories today with a friend he's made at the Seamen's Mission, where he's staying to look for you. Can't you imagine how he must feel, handicapped as he is by his blindness?'

'Look, I have to be sure of my feelings before I can see him,' Jane cried. 'Surely you understand?'

Suzanne said gently, 'I think I do. It's a sticky situation and I sympathize. Alan loves you.'

Jane sighed. 'I know—that's what makes it so tragic. Did you know that he left hospital before he had an operation on his eyes to come to Hong Kong to find me?'

'You mean he was waiting for an operation and he left before they could do it?'

'That's right,' Jane admitted.

'Then why not play along with him?' Suzanne suggested. 'Wait until he's had his operation before you tell him that you don't think you can marry him.'

'But if the operation isn't successful, what then?'

Suzanne smiled, 'I don't think you need to worry on that score. Alan has his pride. Do you honestly think he'd let you make the sacrifice of tying yourself to a blind man for the rest of your life? My guess is that he'll take a lot of convincing that you will want to marry him under those circumstances.'

Jane bit a lip that quivered. 'Thank you,' she said with tears in her eyes. 'There's no problem, is there? Alan is very proud and very stubborn. I'll play along with him until after his operation. I shall know by then what to do.'

The tension between them relaxed, and they began to talk about Hong Kong, that precious commodity water and the strangeness of sleeping under mosquito nets. But they both agreed that it was a wonderful place.

Raoul, with a briefcase under his arm, was leaving when Suzanne walked with Jane to the gate of the house.

'Can I give you a lift back to town?' he asked with a charming lift of the dark brows.

Jane was clearly delighted. 'By all means, if it won't be taking you out of your way,' she said demurely. To Suzanne, she said, 'I'll keep in touch, and thanks for everything.'

Impulsively she stepped forward and kissed Suzanne on her cheek, then followed Raoul to his car. Suzanne watched them go, chiding herself at her disappointment about Raoul's brevity as he shot away. She wondered at Jane's look in his direction as she had accepted his offer of a lift. What kind of a girl was she? Were her actions motivated by the fact that her friend Carol had married a rich man? Had she the same thing in mind for herself? She might even make a play for Raoul. Suzanne's lips curled with derision at the mistaken notion that money could buy happiness. If Raoul had been a poor man she would have followed him gladly barefoot across the world. But he did not love her. If he had ever loved her she had killed that love. If he had. She would never know now.

A little blindly Suzanne made her way to the house to see Tante Jeannette waiting for her on the terrace. Her smile was gentle and kind.

She said, 'How are you this morning? Head better?'

'Fine, thanks,' Suzanne replied, thinking that Jeannette looked a bit peaky. 'Raoul has just left.'

'Yes, I know. I was late getting up this morning,' Tante Jeannette admitted, lifting a pale hand to her head in the manner of someone with a hangover.

Instantly Suzanne was all concern. 'Are you not well?' she asked, going forward to take the older woman's arm and lead her to a wicker chair. 'You look pale,' she added, placing a cushion behind her head as she sank down gratefully into the chair.

'Probably the heat,' Tante Jeannette said apologetically. 'I rarely have headaches, but Sun Yu-Ren is a wizard at mixing a potion at times like this. Maybe I will ask him to make me one later.'

'Why not now? Unless you would rather I sent for the doctor?' Suzanne hovered anxiously. 'If Raoul were here he would insist upon it.'

Tante Jeannette smiled wanly. 'You are as fussy as Raoul,' she said, patting Suzanne's hand. 'I shall take Sun Yu-Ren's potion and lie down in my room.'

Later when she was in bed Suzanne sat beside her waiting for her to go to sleep. It seemed to her that some kind of stress had brought on the bad headache, but she did not probe. One had to remember that Suzanne Dawson was no longer family. Strange how the thought of it hurt so much. Nothing in the whole of her sheltered life had prepared her for the event of Raoul de Brécourt or the de Brécourt family. From the start she had fought against his arrogance, the daredevil twinkle in his dark eyes, the strong-looking hands that had possessed her, caressed her.

'Oh dear!' Tante Jeannette exclaimed suddenly, looking up from her pillows in dismay. 'I had forgotten—we are lunching with Sylvana today. She has asked us to lunch at her house. In fact this is the one day in the week that I always lunch with her and I promised to take you along.'

Suzanne, pleased to see that the colour in her face was better, suggested telephoning Sylvana right away, but she was answered by a sideways movement of Tante Jeannette's head.

She said, 'Sylvana usually goes to her hairdresser this morning, so she will probably be out until just before lunch. In any case she will have gone to enormous trouble to prepare a meal, so we cannot let her down.'

'You mean you want me to go?' Suzanne asked. 'But it wouldn't be right to leave you when you're feeling ill.'

'Nonsense—I am not ill. I am feeling better already. Do go, there's a dear, and make my apologies.'

So promptly at twelve noon Suzanne presented herself at Sylvana's house, to find no one at home. The daily woman was just leaving as she walked into the courtyard, and she was informed that Sylvana had gone out for the day.

Suzanne could not believe that Sylvana would forget a luncheon appointment with one of her closest friends. She thanked the daily woman, who looked at her strangely before going on her way, and turned her steps to the humid heat of the city. There were several things she had promised Tante Jeannette to bring her back from the shops while she was in town and she needed a few things for herself.

She had lunch in town, made her purchases, and it was late afternoon before she was able to set off to catch a tram back to the Peak. She was threading her way through pedestrians when a long shining car drew up silently beside her, and glancing over the top of her parcels she gave a gasp of surprise. Her heart lifted.

'Hop in,' said Raoul, opening the door beside him. 'Give me your parcels.'

He took them from her, tossed them into the spacious back seat of the car and waited for her to settle in beside him. An afternoon shopping in the humid heat plus the surprise of seeing Raoul had sent her face into a rosy glow. The golden hair clung in curly tendrils about her flushed cheeks as the sunlight cut the car into sharp patterns of light and shade. She caught his faint, amused smile and lowered her eyes.

He hesitated before starting the car to let his eyes rove over her slowly, deliberately eyeing the slim figure, the slender arms and shoulders smooth as apricot silk, the silky eyelashes, dark-tipped, and the deep blue of her eyes enhanced by the pretty blue outfit.

'I had forgotten how very blue your eyes are,' he drawled. 'I like your dress. It suits you, brings out the gold of your hair. How is the head?'

'Fine, thanks.' She moved uneasily, feeling his appraisal and wishing that he would lose some of that patronising, amused tolerance which he used when addressing her.

Her flippant answer changed his mood. He said rather curtly, 'Another day taking it easy would not have come amiss. Was it necessary to load yourself up with parcels and shop in the heat? Surely pretty baubles could have waited for another day—and why are you alone?'

He started the car and frowned his disapproval through the windscreen at the dense traffic on the road. Looking at his angry profile, Suzanne was tempted to tell him that most of her purchases were for his aunt, plus a box of her favourite candies and several paperback books she herself had bought for her.

Instead she said rather defiantly, 'You know what girls are.' The thought that he had admitted forgetting what she looked like smarted like an open wound and she added, 'Thanks for reminding me how lucky I am to be able to please myself what I do and what I buy.'

He said quietly, 'I was not aware that I had ever restricted you moneywise. Why have you not used my allowance?'

'I told you I wouldn't use it.'

'Upon reflection,' he murmured slowly, dangerously, 'I was far too lenient with you. I should have put you across my knee at least twice a day and spanked you good and hard. You can blame the gentleman in me for restraining my animal instincts.'

Suzanne bristled with indignation. 'Never mind,' she shot at him. 'You'll know what to do next time you take a wife if she doesn't come up to your expectations. Mind you,' she added for good measure, 'you did have the advantage over me. You did know more about women than I knew about men.'

'One is always learning,' he said dryly.

Suzanne wanted to say that one could learn too late. But she had trespassed on dangerous ground too far as it was, so she changed the subject to one which had been bothering her.

'Tante Jeannette stayed at home today. I think she's unhappy because Oncle Philippe is away so much.'

'Has she said so?'

'Not in so many words, but one can read between the lines.'

'Really? What do you sense about me? If I remember rightly you used to be fairly good with your hunches.'

Suzanne quivered. 'For someone who had forgotten the colour of my eyes your memory is fairly lucid,' she snapped.

'It is,' he agreed with maddening calm. 'It is surprising how the memory sharpens when one begins to resurrect a dead love.'

Suzanne felt the pain like a sword thrust to the heart. 'About ... Tante Jeannette,' she insisted, feeling the urge to go on talking to blot out all feeling, all hurt.

He shot her a sharp glance. 'Nothing you need to concern yourself with, since there will be several changes in the family before the year is out,' he said coolly.

Suzanne was silent. He was telling her to mind her own business as far as the de Brécourt family was concerned. She was no longer part of it.

To her relief Tante Jeannette came to meet them as they left the car. No need to ask if her headache had gone, thought Suzanne. Her eyes were clear and shining and her smile was pain-free.

Suzanne quickly gathered two small parcels from the heap Raoul was gathering from the car and went to greet her aunt. She kissed her cheek.

'Are you better?' she whispered. 'I did all your shopping, and Raoul gave me a lift.'

'I'm much better. Did you have a nice day?'

Suzanne nodded. 'Yes. See you later.'

Swiftly she made her way to her room in a whirl of mixed emotions. So Raoul had definitely decided to marry before the year was out, and his intended could only be Sylvana. She wished him happiness from the bottom of her heart. Her throat felt parched and her feet ached with so much walking around the shops. She would have given anything for a cup of Sun Yu-Ren's tea. But the last thing she wanted was people around her.

By the time she had dressed for dinner that evening Suzanne was feeling more or less calm. A cool emotion had to stifle all others where her dealings with Raoul were concerned. He must no longer have the power to start her senses quivering by his touch, his voice. So she stood with the froth of white organza billowing around her as she learned the anguish of loving without the right to love. The pain of unrequited love was all the more unbearable because she loved him so desperately, and there was nothing she could do. She thought, thank heaven for the company of Tante Jeannette.

But Tante Jeannette had not put in an appearance when she reached the salon. Raoul was by the drinks cabinet. He gave her a swift look which she could not interpret and said very steadily, 'Suzanne on time! This is indeed a surprise. Do sit down while I pour you a drink.'

'Thank you,' she said primly, and sat down.

'How are you feeling?' he asked, handing her a drink. 'You looked hot enough to explode this afternoon when I picked you up.'

Suzanne wished her hand was more steady when she took the glass. But she did manage not to spill the drink. As she waited fervently for Tante Jeannette to put in an appearance, Raoul poured his own drink.

'Well?' he asked, sitting down, leaning back and looking at her, prepared to listen.

'I'm quite all right,' she replied, and took a sip of her drink to steady herself. 'Thanks for the lift.'

Her careless tone implied that she could very well have done without it. He raised a dark brow.

'You are looking better since you came,' he commented, looking at her in that maddening way he had. 'What were you doing, living it up?'

Suzanne looked down at the beautiful cut crystal glass in her hand. It caught facets of light which sparkled like diamonds and she wished futilely that her heart was as hard.

'Something like that,' she replied, determined to go along with him.

Raoul stretched out his legs before him with long-limbed carelessness. His dark hair was as vibrant and alive as the dark eyes echoing the kind of sardonic smile she expected.

He asked, 'Thought any more of inviting your friend here?'

She said frigidly, 'No.'

'Why not?' he persisted lazily.

Suzanne grew more rigid. 'I take it that you're talking about Alan?'

'Yes. Are there others?'

'Other men, you mean? Dozens,' she said tartly.

He was not impressed. 'Then invite them all. The more the merrier.'

Deep blue eyes flashed at him. Steady now, she thought, he's only doing this to rile you. A ripple of apprehension ran along her nerves and to her relief Tante Jeannette chose that moment to drift in the room.

She looked smart and chic in a dress of pearl grey silk.

Suzanne felt very young in white in comparison and wished foolishly that she too was older and more sophisticated.

If Tante Jeannette sensed tension in the air she did not comment on it. Raoul gave her an aperitif as she seated herself near to Suzanne.

'Well, *ma chère*?' she said with a warm smile. 'Did you enjoy your lunch with Sylvana? I must confess that I was disappointed that she did not telephone me later.'

Suzanne moved uneasily in her chair and felt the colour rising in her cheeks. 'I didn't have lunch with Sylvana,' she said.

Jeannette raised finely pencilled brows in disbelief while Raoul, leaning back nonchalantly against the drinks cabinet with his unfinished drink in his hand, smiled sardonically.

'You are embarrassing the child,' he drawled. 'Suzanne probably had lunch with her boy-friend.'

The dark blue eyes flashed a look of dislike his way, then Suzanne said,

'Sylvana was out when I arrived at twelve noon. The daily woman was just leaving, and she said Sylvana was lunching out today.'

Tante Jeannette looked bewildered. 'I simply cannot understand it,' she cried. 'I have always lunched with her on the same day every week. How could she forget?'

Raoul put in evenly, 'I had lunch with Sylvana today. I was going to lunch when I met her, and I was given the impression that she was lunching alone. I am sorry if it upset your plans, but there it is. Sylvana has some explanation, I am sure of it.'

Oh, sure, Suzanne thought bitterly. Sylvana was not English, so was a law unto herself. It was easy to imagine her gliding across the room to Tante Jeannette, fixing her with her dark eyes, and saying softly in her warm throaty voice, 'I completely forgot what day it was. Do forgive me, *cara* Jeannette.'

Sylvana had changed her plans for reasons known only to herself. It might have been a mere whim on her part. But

if she was given to acting so irresponsibly surely Tante
Jeannette, and even Raoul, knew that by now. Jeannette
was not pleased.

The evening meal passed pleasantly. Raoul was at his
sparkling best. He devoted himself to cheering up his aunt
with charm and wit. On the subject of Oncle Philippe he
was sympathetic, promising that things would be very different quite soon. Suzanne was grateful to him. She was
too fond of his aunt to see her so miserable and unhappy.

Later, while sitting replete with the evening meal, Raoul
and Tante Jeannette smoked cigarettes against a background of soft music. Lulled into a false peace, Suzanne was
dismayed when Jeannette left the room for her nightly
telephone call with her husband.

For a while the silence in the room seemed to Suzanne
to be electrically charged. It was maddening to know that
her heart was beating much too quickly and that there was
nothing she could do about it. She hoped the colour burning in her cheeks would go unnoticed. Right now it seemed
futile to fight her consciousness of his nearness and dear-
ness. Later, when she was alone, there would be moments
of self-disgust at her weakness where Raoul was concerned.
The burning issue of the moment was that some day in the
not far distant future he would be gone out of her life for
ever. Beyond that, at this stage, Suzanne did not dare look.

Raoul was the first to break the uneasy silence. He sent
out a line of cigarette smoke ceilingwards and watched it
thoughtfully, then said,

'Why did you not tell me about Tante Jeannette when I
picked you up this afternoon in town?'

She said distantly, 'Because she didn't want any fuss. I
was worried about her if you remember. I had an idea that
the headache was brought on by pressure of some kind.'

'I'll go along with that,' he agreed tolerantly. 'But why be
secretive about going to Sylvana's house to find her out?
You would not have said anything about it if you had not
been asked. Why?'

'Perhaps I thought that Sylvana had a perfectly valid explanation for doing what she did,' she returned.

'It didn't occur to you to return here to report instead of going off on your own?'

'I had some shopping to do.'

Just slightly, his tone sharpened. 'Ah, yes. Mostly for someone else. You never corrected me, did you, on that score when I accused you of doing unnecessary shopping?'

'Why should I, when you're determined to think the worst of me?'

Raoul turned his head to survey her heightened colour soberly. His voice was acid. 'My opinion of you is based on what I know personally.'

She said waveringly, 'Perhaps I deserved that. But I don't care what you think of me one way or the other. I came here at Tante Jeannette's invitation. Had I known you were here I would never have come.'

'But you are here, and you are my responsibility,' he said coolly.

'So you keep saying.' Suzanne felt her calm exterior slipping away and her nerves tightened. 'But you're wrong. I'm nobody's responsibility.'

His tone hardened. 'This going around Hong Kong on your own—you are doing far too much of it.'

She looked at him with stormy blue eyes. 'If you as much as say one word to Tante Jeannette I shall leave on the first flight I can get,' she threatened.

Sarcastically he said, 'I thought you did not want to upset Tante Jeannette?'

Suzanne sighed. 'Yes, I suppose it would upset her. But then my presence here upsets her as well.'

He looked at her sharply. 'Why should you say that?'

Suzanne could not meet his eyes. 'Because ... because of our marriage,' she managed weakly.

He regarded her quizzically. 'I do not quite comprehend.'

'What do you not comprehend?'

Tante Jeannette had drifted back into the room and she smiled down at Suzanne.

'You are wanted on the telephone, *chérie*. Someone named Alan Edge.'

'Thanks.'

Suzanne sprang to her feet, eager to escape from Raoul and his searching gaze. Alan could not wait to tell her about Jane calling to see him at the Seamen's Mission. Suzanne was so relieved that there was a happy lilt to her voice that lifted it on to a brighter note. No mention was made of Jane visiting her that morning, so Suzanne concluded that it would be better not to mention it. Far better that Alan should think that Jane was as eager to meet him as he was to meet her.

Alan went on to say that he would like her to spend the following evening with them. They planned to go out to one of the floating restaurants. His friend from the Seamen's Mission would make a foursome if she would come.

'That would be lovely. Of course I'll be delighted to come.' Suzanne could not keep the pleasure she felt at the suggestion out of her voice. To get away from Raoul for an evening would be something to look forward to. 'Where shall I meet you?' she added breathlessly.

Alan said that his friend was hiring a car and they would all call for her at seven o'clock. They talked for some time, Suzanne sharing his joy.

'I'm so happy for you, Alan,' she ended. 'I shall look forward to seeing you tomorrow evening.'

As she put down the telephone Suzanne turned to see Raoul strolling towards her. He was watching the frank enchantment of her face when suddenly she lifted her blue eyes to his. Their gaze held and she quickly lowered her lashes over eyes that hungered with emptiness.

'You look positively radiant,' he mocked. 'I'm curious about this friend of yours since he can make you look so happy.' He pushed his hands into the pockets of his dinner jacket, and regarded her with hard eyes. 'What am I to expect, an overnight whirlwind courtship and marriage?'

Suzanne clenched her hands in the folds of her organza

dress. She retreated a little, feeling his magnetism, as much under his spell as she had been since meeting him again. Disconcerted, she put a hand to her face, felt it burn, and said heatedly, 'You tell me, since you know so much about me!'

There was a silence during which she ventured a look up at his face. His eyes were kind as they searched her face.

He said with feeling, 'I owe you an apology. I should not have spoken to you as I did just now. After all, we have our separate lives to get on with as we will. Care for a short stroll in the garden?'

Suzanne panicked. To walk with him in the garden, to be aware of him to the extent of feeling desire for him well in her treacherous heart—she could not.

'Tante Jeannette . . .' she began nervously.

'Gone to her room,' he finished for her.

Facing the inevitable, she found herself walking beside him into the scented night air. There was something about the magnificent night sky, the breathtaking view of millions of lights over the harbour below that brought the tears to her eyes. In that moment all she could think of was the past, the passion and the depth of their relationship through marriage. If in the next few moments Raoul were to take her into his arms, she knew she would not have the strength nor the inclination to resist him. The thought frightened her, but somehow she managed to walk beside him like someone detached as he seemed to be.

Presently he said, 'This man Alan—are you in love with him?'

Suzanne told herself that he was probing because he wanted to know the situation as it stood between them. Regarding her as his responsibility, he was anxious to have her off his hands before he carried out his own plans for the future. The burden of her own unhappiness weighed down on her, forcing tears to her eyes until the harbour lights danced in a coloured haze.

His eyes were inscrutable, intent upon her face, and she

blinked the tears away, unaware that the soft muted light fell gently on her hair and emphasised its golden sheen. The faint night breeze, pine-sweet from the heights, wafted poignantly across the pale blur of her face.

She said huskily, 'That surely is my business. In any case, I've only just met him.'

'That isn't what I asked.' His tones were sardonic. 'Time does not exist when certain people meet for the first time. There is a kind of chemical reaction between them that fuses them together. Love, physical attraction, call it what you will.'

Bleakly, she said, 'And you, of course, are speaking from experience?'

'Are you asking me if I have ever been in love?' he asked softly, dangerously. His eyes, moving over her, bared her soul. 'There are some things a man does not disclose to anyone except, perhaps, to the woman he loves above all else. I want you to be happy. Isn't that enough?'

Her head said, Let him think that I love Alan—it was better that than he should discover where her heart really lay. Suddenly for no reason at all, she began to laugh. He was not to know that she was desperately unhappy, that she had either to laugh or cry.

'You really are funny,' she said. 'We're divorced, remember?'

Very quietly, he said, 'I am not likely to forget it with you around. I asked you to come outdoors so that we can talk.'

'What about? We have nothing to discuss, Raoul.'

'I beg to differ,' he answered firmly. 'Here you are unaccompanied in a place like Hong Kong and you expect me to do nothing about it. Strange as it may seem to you, your future is of vital importance to ... us.'

Suzanne stiffened. Was he including Sylvana in that last little word? And that slight hesitation before he had said it was not at all like him. With eyes sharpened by love she saw that he looked immensely strong and lean ... too lean.

Was he worried about something? She could hardly think he worried about her. Tante Jeannette? No. He was going to put things right there. That left Sylvana. More than anything Suzanne wanted him to be happy. Gradually she softened.

'Aren't you taking my presence here too seriously? I'm well able to take care of myself. Furthermore, you created this situation to which you're giving so much thought,' she said lightly.

He let this go. 'Have you ever wondered why I encouraged you to visit Tante Jeannette?' he queried. 'I did it to bring you and me closer—I thought you would feel that you really belonged in my family. But it meant nothing to you, did it?'

Suzanne forced herself to be flippant. 'If you're under the impression that I expect anything of you because of ... our former relationship you couldn't be more wrong. It's all over, Raoul—you know that; I know that. Go back to Paris and your French cooking. Or is it Sylvana and Italian pasta?'

To her horror she felt her control slipping. She would either have to collapse on his chest in a flood of tears or go quickly. The next moment she had fled.

CHAPTER EIGHT

ON the terrace overlooking the Chinese garden, the sun was already hot on Suzanne's bare shoulders. The pretty cotton sun-dresses she had worn when abroad were now becoming second nature. Returning later to the colder weather of London was something she could not bear to think about, but it must be faced, and soon.

Raoul had gone out before she had come down to breakfast. There were two letters beside her plate from England. One was from her solicitors informing her that the matter of her rescuing two children from a life of almost total illiteracy in order to give them a good education had been settled. Her cheque had been gratefully received. The second letter from Oncle Philippe was covered with postmarks, having followed her around for the past twelve months. He had written it during a short visit to London on business.

In it he had sent condolences on the death of her father and put himself at her service if ever she needed help in any way. In the meantime he believed that Jeannette was writing to invite her to stay with her in Hong Kong. He hoped she would go, and he asked her to keep in touch.

Tenderly, Suzanne realised that his letter, along with that of Tante Jeannette, had been correspondence she had missed when she went abroad. Dear Oncle Philippe, she thought, and gave the letter to her aunt to read as she joined her for breakfast.

'Philippe is very fond of you, *ma chère*,' she said after reading the letter. 'You really should have let us know that you were going abroad and at least have left us your address. None of us had any idea where you had gone after you lost your father.'

117

Suzanne thought how easy it would be to talk to this sweet-natured woman, to lay her troubles at her feet. So she told her about her father's illness, her own anguish, and the desire to go away from everything and everybody to sort out her disordered life. Beyond that she did not go; she was not sure how much of what she told would go back to Raoul.

Jeannette, listening compassionately, realised that Suzanne had gone through her testing time with no one to help soften the blows. She would have liked to smooth away the hurt and fears, the future troubles that would, without a doubt, beset a young woman who had looks and money. But Suzanne was better not looking back on the past. Like Raoul, she had to make a future all her own. Philippe, like Raoul, was taken by Suzanne's charm and beauty. She was young and therefore in need of protection. Philippe and Raoul were two of a kind in believing that a woman needed cherishing. She herself was not a hard woman, neither was she cynical, but she had seen her nephew go through a traumatic experience ending in divorce and she had no desire to see it repeated.

'Have you made any plans for the future?' she asked kindly.

Suzanne shook her head. Something dark had descended on the light of the morning. She sensed her companion's tenseness, and doubted if it had been brought on through seeing Philippe's letter when she had not seen the writer for so long. Did her aunt really want her to go so soon? A lump stuck in her throat and threatened to choke her. But before she could form any words with lips that were strangely stiff, the sound of a car throbbing into silence outside the gates alerted her.

The husky, accented voice came clearly to them as Sylvana drifted across their line of vision. The rings on her fingers caught the sun as she approached with outstretched hands to greet her friend with disarming candour.

'Poor *cara* Jeannette!' she cried. 'Please forgive me for

disturbing you so early, but I felt I had to come to apologise for letting you down yesterday. How could I have forgotten our weekly date which I look forward to so much? Yet I did, and you must blame Raoul for it.' She laughed as if the whole matter was too absurd to be important. Suzanne she ignored completely for the moment. 'I could not resist an invitation to have lunch with him.'

'Why not?' Suzanne could not help saying, feeling rather sickened at what looked like a theatrical performance.

'Why not?' Sylvana echoed, dramatically giving Suzanne her attention. 'I have yet to meet a woman who could resist Raoul's charm.' Her smile suddenly became coy. 'Besides, we had things to talk about. Raoul is helping me in one or two business ventures among other things.'

Jeannette said without malice, 'I forgive you, Sylvana. It is Suzanne who was put out by the forgetfulness. I did not accompany her to keep our date. She went alone because I was indisposed.'

'Jeannette, and I was not to know. How are you, *mia cara*? Not ill, I trust?'

Did Suzanne trace a genuine thread of feeling running through the dulcet tones? In any case, she decided, Sylvana was too absurd, too likeable to take offence. She had her deepest sympathy if she was enamoured of Raoul.

She said, 'Tante Jeannette had a headache, and no harm was done. I stayed in town to do some shopping. So don't distress yourself over the matter.' She smiled. 'I forgive you too.'

Sylvana turned swiftly from Suzanne to Jeannette. 'Is she not sweet, this little English rose whom I admire so much?' she cried. 'How good it is to know two such nice, wonderful people!'

'Suzanne is not one to bear malice,' said Jeannette.

'That is good to hear. I could not bear it if we were not friends.' Sylvana bent down to kiss Suzanne's soft cheek. 'I must make amends.'

Jeannette smiled. 'Then you can begin by taking Suzanne

out. I have several appointments today.'

Sylvana looked delighted and Jeannette added dryly, 'Raoul insists that the child does not go out alone. So you will look after her and bring her back here yourself.'

Suzanne was aware then that some conversation concerning her had taken place between Jeannette and Raoul. Since the other woman's query as to her future plans she had felt on edge, and the arrival of Sylvana had done nothing to assuage it. Indeed Sylvana seemed to have increased the influence over herself of the absent Raoul with the same tormenting thoughts returning to nag her. What were Sylvana and he to each other?

'Suzanne, come,' cried Sylvana on a gay note. 'Let us go out on the town. Instead of China tea in dainty little cups we shall have coffee and talk about the things which delight women. Then we shall take lunch in some delightful restaurant.'

'With Italian food as a speciality?' Suzanne put in.

'Ah, yes,' Sylvana gurgled. 'You will come as you are in your pretty sun-dress.'

Suzanne really enjoyed her day with her effervescent companion. As she had promised, they called for midmorning coffee at a coffee-house overlooking the harbour, lunched at an Italian restaurant and generally discussed the current women's fashions and how becoming Chinese cheongsams were on the Chinese women.

And all the time Suzanne was thinking how hard it was to resist this volatile Italian with her warm-hearted exuberance. Small wonder that Raoul had been captivated by her.

She was dressing to go out that evening when Jeannette wandered into her room to watch her dress. The lovely Chinese cheongsam in greys, blacks and emerald lay on the bed. Sylvana had persuaded her to buy it because it was so beautiful, and Tante Jeannette gazed at it in admiration.

'I cannot wait to see you in it,' she cried. 'With your slender figure it should be perfect.'

Suzanne, looking very sweet and youthful in exquisite underwear, reached out for the dress and put it on.

'The colouring is just right with your golden hair,' Jeannette remarked. She was thinking that if Raoul could see his ex-wife now he would be hard put not to take her in his arms and kiss her lovely mouth. For with her flowing hair a pale cloud around her proud young head, her slender young body so seductive in the cheongsam, she was a true femme fatale—and he was nothing if not a man.

So it was with a mixture of relief and uneasiness that Jeannette saw Suzanne leave with the three young people in the car that had arrived on time to collect her.

Suzanne was normally of a happy disposition and young enough to forget for an evening the depressing thoughts of the future, so she thoroughly enjoyed herself.

Alan's friend, a very attractive young man with red hair and an engaging grin, fell for her on sight.

'Wow!' he exclaimed as he sprang from the car to help her in beside him. 'Why didn't you tell me, Alan, what a treat lay in store for me? What a bird!'

Jane, sitting in the back of the car with Alan, said in envy, 'I love your cheongsam. I have one not so pretty as that to take back with me when I go home.'

Suzanne's companion sat looking at her for several seconds before he introduced himself.

He said, 'My name is Leroy Stone. My friends call me Lee.'

'And I'm Suzanne Dawson,' she said. 'My friends call me Suzanne.'

Lee sat staring at her for several seconds as if mesmerised until Jane said very softly from her back seat, 'Don't you think you'd better start the car, Lee?'

They all laughed as Lee gave a start and turned to the wheel. The evening was a success from the beginning, with everyone determined to enjoy themselves. On the boat going out to the floating restaurant someone played a guitar and they all sang.

They dined and danced with healthy abandon and it was a very happy quartet that returned to the harbour at a late hour. Suzanne was taken back to the Peak before they dropped Jane off and it was a happy singing crowd stopped outside the house at the gates.

It was to be the last time that Suzanne would see them, as Lee was leaving the following day to reboard his ship and Alan was going home with Jane.

Suzanne said her goodbyes to them and Lee walked with her through the gates to the house. He walked with the rolling gait of a sailor and Suzanne compared it with Raoul's natural ease of movement. With Raoul the whole of him moved with fluid grace, and Suzanne thought angrily that he had spoiled her for anyone else.

The house was lighted up, but she could see no one on the terrace or in the garden.

Lee said, 'This has been one of the happiest nights of my life. I've thoroughly enjoyed myself.'

'So have I,' Suzanne agreed, looking up into his nice serious face. 'But don't let's treat it seriously. One should never propose by moonlight. Daylight is a much more sensible down-to-earth time.' She laughed. 'You just look as if you're about to pop the question, Lee!'

She was far too sensitive not to be aware of the feeling she had aroused in her companion during the evening. To her it had all been harmless fun, but with Lee she was not too sure.

'How did you guess?' he asked. 'You can't blame me for reaching a bit higher, can you? I know you're not my sort, but it doesn't stop me from falling for you. I wonder, would you write to me?'

Suzanne shook her head. 'I'm sorry. I don't know where I shall be in the future, and neither do you, so let's leave it at that, shall we?' she said gently.

He nodded in a hurt kind of way and Suzanne, full of compassion, reached up to kiss him.

The house was very quiet when she went to the main

salon to see if Tante Jeannette was still up. The wall lights
were on and there was a stream of fresh air coming across
the room from the open windows leading out on to the
terrace. Was it possible that Jeannette could be out there?
She paused uncertainly with a feeling of apprehension at
the thought of an intruder. Then gathering all her courage,
she moved swiftly across the room and cannoned violently
into a hard unyielding figure coming into the room. Arms
like steel bands closed around her and she fought against
them.

'Let me go!' she cried in a muffled voice against the wide
chest.

Her heart was beating hard and she was terrified.

'*Doucement*,' a familiar deep voice said softly. 'No one is
going to hurt you.'

Trembling from head to toe, she lifted her head to gaze
up at the mocking dark face above her. She was still crushed
against him and her heart was thudding into him.

'Oh, it's you! I—I thought it was an intruder.' Her lips
were trembling so much that she caught them between
small white even teeth. 'How dare you frighten me like
that?' she cried. 'And let me go at once!'

'I think you had better sit down,' Raoul said grimly. 'I'll
get you a drink.'

'I—I don't want ... to ... to sit down,' she stammered.
'I'm going to ... bed.'

His arms slackened their grip around her, but he kept a
grip on one slender arm.

'Sit down,' he said sternly, and steered her to a comfortable chair.

Suzanne's legs were trembling so much she was glad to
sink down into soft upholstery, and she leaned back to
close her eyes.

Futile to tell herself that an intruder might have been
easier to handle than her ex-husband.

He was saying, 'I did not run into you—you ran into me.
Don't tell me that you could not wait to see me again.'

The blue eyes flew open. 'That will be the day,' she jibed, on breath regained. 'I thought you were away.'

'I returned an hour ago.'

He was bending over a low table uncovering a tray to pour out hot liquid from a flask into a cup.

'Drink this. Be careful, it is hot.' She stared at it and he said impatiently, 'Come on. A hot drink is good for shock.' A hint of malice crept into the deep tones as he added, 'It should be good. Your devoted slave Sun Yu-Ren left it for you.'

But her hand was not yet steady enough to hold the cup firmly and Raoul retained his hold until he had put down the flask. His warm fingers closed her own around the cup and the contact did nothing to steady her. He was too close, dangerously so.

'Come on,' he teased. 'Drink. It isn't the first time I've helped you with a drink.'

He was kneeling beside her now and smiling. Her heart was a heavy aching torment. The drink was a face-saver, a help to her sinking pride.

She drank from the cup held persistently to her lips, then pushed it away. Raoul straightened to his full height, put down the cup and said,

'You have only yourself to blame for what happened just now. Had you not been so engrossed in your companion in a tender leavetaking you would have seen me on the terrace or, at least, the glow from the cigarette I was smoking.' He paused and in the soft glow of the wall lights, his dark eyes took on a merciless gleam. His tones were savage. 'Did you exchange partners with Jane for the evening?'

Suzanne stared at him in amazement. 'Why should you say that?'

He moved wide shoulders indifferently. 'Jane was one of the friends who called for you this evening, was she not?'

'Yes, she was. You quizzed her when you gave her that lift to town just as you quiz Tante Jeannette about me, didn't you?'

'I have quizzed no one. Furthermore Jane told me nothing about herself except that she was a dancer out of a job. I offered her a lift to town because I was going that way,' he said coldly.

'Then why should you ask if we'd changed partners?'

'Because I heard you call the young man who brought you home Lee.'

Her lip curled contemptuously. 'How you must have enjoyed spying on me!'

He said angrily, 'Will you stop accusing me of doing anything so underhand! I arrived back here an hour or so ago to find Tante Jeannette waiting up for you. Sun Yu-Ren was about to bring in a tray for when you returned. I sent them to bed when I heard that you were not expected back until late as you'd been picked up to dine out with a party of three young people.'

'And you sent Sun Yu-Ren to bed because you were going to wait until I came in? I ... I ... never knew such high-handedness!' Her swift intake of breath was one of pure anger. 'Well, you can relax, because I'm leaving on the first flight I can get!'

Raoul was not put out in the slightest. His mouth curved maddeningly at the corners.

'I hardly think you will do that when you hear that someone who is very fond of you will be here quite shortly,' he drawled.

Suzanne wrinkled a youthfully smooth brow. Then her expression cleared miraculously.

'Not Oncle Philippe?' she cried.

'The very same,' he replied. 'That is all I am prepared to say at the moment. We want it to be a surprise for his wife.'

He strolled across to the French windows and locked them. Then he turned to face her.

'By the way,' he said, 'who was the young man who brought you home this evening?'

Her prickles rose. Obstinacy was once more back in her

face. 'What is it to do with you? He's quite respectable,' she cried.

Raoul said savagely, 'You pick a sailor up in Hong Kong and say he is respectable? What do you know about him? Don't be so naïve!'

'But ... but how did you know he was a sailor?' she gasped.

'Who could not know?' His tones were filled with distaste.

He gestured with a lean brown hand. 'That remark was not meant to be derogatory in any way. I have the highest regard for sailors. But Hong Kong is hardly the place to make friendships with people about whom you know practically nothing.' He strolled towards her, frowning disapprovingly. 'You have to remember that this island simply teems with drug peddlers and all other kinds of unsavoury pursuits. I see no reason why you did not invite him in. I am sure he would have appreciated the hospitality offered.'

Suzanne stiffened. She said coldly, 'You seem to forget that this is not my house and that I am only a guest here at Tante Jeannette's invitation. For all I knew she might have had other guests here for the evening. As it happens, you were here.'

Raoul pushed his hands into his pockets and his mouth thinned. Sarcastically, he said, 'And I am so formidable that you could not face me? Tell me,' sardonically, 'did you know I was here when you kissed your sailor goodnight?'

His savage tones rasped her nerves. The colour gradually ebbed from her face, leaving her white and trembling.

'What do you mean?' she whispered hoarsely.

'It occurred to me that you did see me on the terrace and you kissed your sailor goodnight for my benefit.' His dark eyes smouldered with anger. 'Either that or you are more liberal with your favours than you used to be.'

Colour came back slowly to her face, staining her cheeks

to a wild rose, and she sprang to her feet to face him angrily.

'How dare you?' she cried. 'It's bad enough insinuating that you matter to me at all, but to accuse me of promiscuity is the last straw! Had I known you were here I would have gone straight to my room.'

He said tightly, 'You insist on treating me as an enemy. I wonder why? You cannot possibly be afraid of me?'

Suzanne laughed. But she began to move away from him just the same as she regarded him in increasing animosity.

'Again you are insinuating that you are important to me,' she said haughtily.

With her face raised and her golden hair swinging back she looked sweet and breathtakingly lovely. The deep rose colour in her cheeks enhanced the blue of her eyes, and Raoul determinedly removed his gaze and turned slightly away.

But Suzanne was the more uncomfortable of the two. She gripped her hands in a horrible dread that Raoul would seize her in his arms and thus discover her secret, that she loved him. He did not, however, and her anger evaporated. All the same she had to steel her shrinking sensibilities to act naturally.

He mocked her disdainful attitude. 'Why move away from me if you are not afraid?'

Suzanne knew she was on dangerous ground. 'I can't see any point in continuing this conversation. I'm going to bed.'

The dark eyes raked her face mercilessly as if to bare her soul. Then he moved in front of her, deliberately barring her way.

Suzanne trembled, wondering how to meet his arrogance. She was totally unprepared for the hand that shot out to grip her wrist. His hold was as searing as hot metal and her bones felt as if they were melting in some forest fire. She had neither the desire nor the strength to resist.

Tense and unsmiling, he said tersely, 'You have not answered my question. Are you afraid of me? Heaven knows I never gave you any cause to be.'

Suzanne wanted to say, How could any woman be afraid of the man she loves? But how could she confess to a love that would not even touch him?

'No, I'm not afraid of you.' She spoke so low that he could scarcely hear her.

The anger died from his face leaving it cool and hard. When he spoke it was with an impersonal harshness.

'I have an idea, I do not know why, that you think I never loved you. You believe that or not as you like, *ma chère*. I am admitting nothing, but I will not have you treating me like a leper. Is that understood?'

Suzanne kept her head bent. 'You make me feel uneasy—afraid to ask you anything. I have this guilt complex—and it's hard to feel guilty and friendly with a person at the same time. I'm sorry, Raoul, I really am. I should never have come to Hong Kong.'

'On the contrary. It is fortunate that you have, because there is one thing I mean to teach you before you go, and that is to trust me.'

He released her hand to force up her chin with a firm forefinger.

There was a brief keen scrutiny of her face before his eyes rested upon her mouth. His lips came down on hers in a crushing kiss ... he felt the soft sweetness of her lips, felt the tremor through her slender frame as she responded.

When he let her go, he said thickly, 'That is a seal on our friendship. What have we left in life if we regard each other as enemies?'

Palpitating and utterly bereft, Suzanne stared up at him before fleeing from the room.

Tante Jeannette awakened her the following morning with a cup of tea.

'It is eleven o'clock, *chérie*,' she said. 'We decided to let you sleep in because it was late when you went to bed.'

'Goodness, it can't be that late! I must have overslept.'

Suzanne pushed herself up in bed, pushed the golden hair behind her ears and looked apologetically at her. 'Thanks for the tea. But you ought not to have bothered.'

Tante Jeannette sat down on the bed. 'I came to waken you,' she said. 'There is a young man downstairs who wants to see you. I think it is one of the friends who came for you last evening.'

Suzanne hastily swallowed the tea. It would be Lee, of course, he had come to say goodbye. But she had hardly expected him to come since their parting the previous evening had been final on her part.

Tante Jeannette added, 'There is no hurry. You have time to wash and dress.' She noted the dark shadows beneath the blue eyes. 'Did you not sleep well, or did you enjoy yourself far too much last evening?'

Suzanne managed a smile. 'If I have a hangover it will be from staying in bed beyond my usual time of getting up!'

'I waited up for you last evening. Then Raoul returned unexpectedly and sent me to bed. He wanted to know whom you had gone out with—he was concerned about you being out so late.'

Did it help to know that he had been uneasy about her? Suzanne was too numb to work it out.

She said wearily, 'I seem to be causing concern when I don't intend to.'

Tante Jeannette patted her hand. 'No, no, *ma chère*. Raoul had to wait up last evening for a long-distance telephone call.'

Suzanne's lips moved mechanically. 'Nice to know that he lost no sleep over me.'

Tante Jeannette took the empty cup. 'Would you rather I sent your friend away? Perhaps you would rather rest in bed until lunch?'

'Oh no! He's leaving today, so I must see him.'

Tante Jeannette stood up and Suzanne reached out for a wrap on a chair near to the bed, swung herself from between the bedclothes and shrugged into it. Then slipping her feet into soft mules, she made her way to the door.

But the young man waiting for her on the terrace was not Lee. It was Alan, a far different Alan from the one she was accustomed to seeing. He looked taller, more upright, and his face was different too. His eyes were not so tired-looking and he had no white stick with him.

Suzanne ran forward to greet him eagerly. 'Alan!' she smiled up at him, taking his hands with a delighted cry. 'You can see!' She began to laugh. 'You know, I've just discovered something. You're quite nice-looking.'

'Thanks,' Alan grinned, and bent down to kiss her hands. 'You're quite something yourself.'

'But how did it happen? Do sit down and tell me.'

She drew him forward to a chair and took the one next to him at a wicker table.

He said. 'I opened my eyes this morning expecting a hangover after our night out and the most wonderful thing happened—I could see! Mind you, the surgeon warned me that my sight could come back. I didn't believe him. I thought he was just saying it to bolster my morale.'

'And what does Jane say?'

'She doesn't know yet. You're the first person I've told except for a long-distance telephone call to the surgeon in London. He wants to see me right away when I get back.'

'But why me, Alan? I haven't done much for you.'

He took her hands warmly in his. 'You did a lot for me. You encouraged me to go on searching for Jane when I was about to give up. Besides, I wanted to see you before we went back, not only to thank you but to see if my mental picture of you was as true as the actual one.'

Suzanne laughed up at him with the thought that something really good had come out of her visit to Hong Kong after all.

'And is it?' she teased.

He nodded and squeezed her hands. 'Perfect, except that your hair is pure gold and your eyes a much deeper blue than I could ever imagine.'

'Compliments so early in the morning!' A small ripple of laughter left her throat and Raoul, entering the salon to gaze at their two heads silhouetted against the brightness of the morning sun, stopped in his tracks.

Alan said simply, 'I could fling compliments right, left and centre this morning. You've no idea how beautiful the world has become to me in these last few hours.'

'You've made my day too. I'm sure you're dying to tell your good news to Jane. What about Lee?'

'He sailed early this morning,' he told her. 'He fell heavily for you, by the way.' Rather shyly, he went on, 'He isn't your kind. He isn't the marrying type, but I really think he would have had a go at it with you.' He gave her hands a final squeeze and said reluctantly. 'I must go. Our plane leaves at four this afternoon.'

'Good morning,' said Raoul smoothly. 'Won't you introduce me to your friend, Suzanne?'

Alan had risen to his feet and Suzanne followed suit. 'Certainly,' she said coolly. 'Alan, this is Raoul de Brécourt. Raoul, Alan Edge, a friend of mine from London.'

They shook hands. Raoul was charmingly polite. 'So you are leaving Hong Kong? I wish you a pleasant journey.'

Suzanne said hurriedly, 'I'll walk with you to the gate, Alan.'

She thrust her arm through his and drew him away without looking at Raoul.

'Good-looking chap, splendid air about him beneath the stamp of success, the kind of bloke who makes everything he wears seem correct,' Alan commented. 'But I don't think he liked me much.'

Suzanne said lightly, 'I wouldn't let that worry you. He doesn't like me either. I'm here at the invitation of his aunt. Besides, he knows nothing about you and there wasn't time to explain.'

They had paused at the gate. Alan said. 'I'll never forget you. Suzanne. I might see you again some day. Bless you—and thanks for everything.'

Suzanne, feeling near to tears, reached up to draw down his head to kiss him.

'Take care,' she said. 'I have a feeling that everything is going to come right for you from now on. Sometimes troubled incidents are a part of the jigsaw that's needed to fit the good things of life together.'

Suzanne walked slowly back to the house, knowing that Jane would not get in touch with her before she left the island. The girl would never want Alan to know how near she came to deserting him in his hour of need. Suzanne only hoped that she would make him a good wife.

Raoul had gone when she reached the salon, but Tante Jeannette was there, arranging flowers in a Ming vase.

'Has your friend gone?' she asked, tweaking a bloom into place, then stepping back to admire it. 'These flowers are from Philippe. He sends them every day that he is away. Chinese gardens are like the Japanese in their fondness for ornamental rocks, trees and waterfalls—artistic, but rather bleak to a lover of flowers.'

Suzanne paused. Strange how bleak and empty the morning seemed to be now that Alan had gone. She had the feeling that Tante Jeannette was making conversation for its own sake.

She said, 'Is Raoul going to marry Sylvana?'

Jeannette's delicate eyebrows shot up in surprise at the unexpected question. But her smile was friendly enough.

'I could not say what Raoul's plans are. If he is planning to marry Sylvana then all I can say is that she will be a very lucky girl.'

'Would you like her to be one of the family?'

Jeannette shrugged. 'Well, I do know her fairly well. She is inclined to be unpredictable at times, but we should get on well enough, I suppose. Have you made any plans for the future yourself?'

'No.'

Jeannette laughed lightly. 'Never mind, my invitation to visit us when we settle down again in Paris still stands.

Meanwhile I am having a small dinner party this evening, and I would like to discuss it with you. Just a few friends, you understand?'

Suzanne nodded, wondering how much longer she could bear the present situation. If only Oncle Philippe would come quickly! She could leave then with no queries as to why she was going so soon.

CHAPTER NINE

IT was all so beautiful, Suzanne thought with a sigh. The scene from her window was one depicting the ageless limit of time. The sea and sky were a translucent blue and the haze drifting across the harbour created a dreamlike quality of silence. A deep emotion gripped her throat, surprising her by its alien quality. In the soft evening light the aura of romance shrouding this strange and beautiful island was almost tangible.

She thought with painful intensity of Raoul, whom she had not seen all day but who was expected back that night with two friends to dinner. Her thoughts centred on all the coiled-spring vitality which he had disciplined into his work. Did he also sense the strange influence of this exotic island? Was he in love with Sylvana?

Sylvana. Suzanne knew that she ought to feel grateful to her rival for acting as a kind of brake upon her own emotions where Raoul was concerned. The brief instances in their marriage when he had shared moments with her in which he had revealed some of the workings of his brilliant mind taunted—the deep cadence of his voice, the intelligent sparkle in those dark eyes, the deep chuckle. All these things had combined to make him an unforgettable figure. No wonder he had been the biggest factor in her life, a powerful compelling figure which, in the flesh, undermined all her resolutions to put him out of her life and in the past where he belonged.

The sound of a car arriving blotted out the treacherous reflections. Then Sylvana drifted into view alone. She moved gracefully across the courtyard in a scarlet evening gown topped by a short fur cape. A chill descended upon Suzanne. Where Raoul was concerned his ex-wife Suzanne belonged to the past, while Sylvana was very much in the present. If there were obstacles between him and Sylvana they were not of his making, and Suzanne had to remember that. She must also remember that as his ex-wife she had no claim on him whatsoever.

She stood a little longer in the poignant sweet beauty of the scene, tinged now with a sense of bitterness that must always be a part of her love for him.

Her appearance in the doorway of the salon had not been intentionally timed to make an impact, but make an impact it did. Raoul was there looking very fit, very handsome. His lean-loined vigour made the stocky, shorter man beside him look much more mature, although he could not have been more than thirty. They were talking to Sylvana over their drinks. Some distance away stood Tante Jeannette with a tall slim man in his fifties, very much a de Brécourt with his dark striking features and leashed vitality.

'Oncle Philippe!' Suzanne murmured, and she gazed towards him with a beautiful expression of joy mingled with ecstatic surprise. In that instant all eyes were turned upon her. The colour rushed to her fine-boned face. She stood poised for an instant exuding an air of delicacy with the light catching the dark tips of eyelashes as golden as the shining, swinging hair. Her creamy skin suffused with colour, her lips pinkly fresh, Suzanne was unaware of her own attractions in the dress she had picked at random. As she ran forward the swirling skirt of the cream dress with its band of embroidery looked almost ethereal.

'Oncle Philippe!' she cried with a delighted smile that held no hint of coquetry. 'I'm sorry I didn't reply to your letter, but I've only just received it after all this time.'

'Suzanne, *mignonne*!' Philippe smiled as he embraced her to plant a kiss on each of her flushed cheeks. 'You are more beautiful than ever!'

Suzanne blinked back the tears as she smiled up at this man who was so poignantly like Raoul would be in later years. The white wings of hair at his temples gave him a distinguished appearance, but she thought he looked tired.

'Allow me to present one of our English representatives,' Raoul put in firmly. 'Miles Payne, Suzanne.'

'Dawson,' Suzanne added quickly as she recovered. For a few moments she had forgotten the other guests until Raoul's words jerked her into remembering.

She smiled and offered her hand. Miles Payne was brown-haired, with hazel eyes, his features unremarkable yet strangely attractive. His glance was steady, his handshake firm, with the kindness in his expression adding enormously to his charm. Instinctively Suzanne felt that she had found a new friend.

'French?' queried Miles while retaining a loose hold on her fingers.

Suzanne laughed. 'English,' she confessed, adding, as she noticed him studying her ringless hands, 'Actually I'm di ...'

'Allow me.'

She turned to find Raoul offering her a drink, his face maddeningly enigmatic. She felt his disapproval over something and could not for the life of her understand why he eyed her so darkly. Then he was giving his attention to Sylvana, who drawled something about her looking sweet enough to eat and they drifted into conversation.

The dinner was a tribute to Sun Yu-Ren's culinary skills. There was sweet corn, egg and shark's fin soup, fried quail, diced chicken with walnuts, young tender pork with rice, salad with mixed vegetables and a desert of mixed honey-dew and watermelon. As each of the delicately flavoured dishes for which the Chinese are so famous were served Suzanne found it impossible for her palate to do full justice to them. She was too aware of Raoul and Sylvana seated opposite to her at the table. She had wondered if Raoul had brought Miles to dinner for her benefit in order that she would not feel the odd one out. It did not help when she learned that Miles was to stay for a few days as their guest.

And while Oncle Philippe teased and Tante Jeannette

looked sublimely happy and content, Suzanne told herself
that she could now leave without the maximum of fuss.
After being away from each other for such long intervals
it was only natural that they would not want a third party
hanging around, especially Raoul's ex-wife. After all, he
was quite happy with his new love Sylvana who dressed
superbly, was very entertaining, and very much taken with
him. It hurt terribly to know that Raoul would forget her
as he had done before, once she had gone. Later, they
would all be returning to their beloved France. And who
better to accompany them than Sylvana who, besides being
loved by Raoul, was also Jeannette's friend?

The waning light of a summer's day met them when they
all retired after the evening meal to the terrace to sit in a
semi-circle facing the garden. The men smoked, Sylvana
desultorily, Jeannette and Suzanne not at all. The fragrance
of nocturnal scents from the grounds mingled with the
aroma of tobacco as they discussed the island.

Miles agreed with Raoul that Hong Kong was not the
shopping paradise it was, adding in a jocular vein that for all
that it was as romantic as ever it had been. Raoul agreed,
with such a self-derisory note in his deep voice that Sylvana
took him up on it.

She blew out a channel of smoke with a dainty air. 'Raoul
a romantic?' she cried. 'I never thought I would see the day.
Could I be in part responsible for it?'

She shone up at Raoul provocatively and Suzanne, from
her seat between Jeannette and Miles with Sylvana on his
other side and Raoul, like Philippe, on either end of the
semi-circle, quivered at the look in his dark eyes. Sylvana
was exhilarating company and fun to be with. Raoul would
certainly agree with that, Suzanne thought miserably. There
was no reason why she should not use her own wiles on
Miles, but she was too honest to pretend a feeling she did
not have. It was like turning a sword in a mortal wound to
watch them together, but she had no choice. And if Raoul
was happy that was all she wanted.

Later, as they were all about to go to their respective

rooms, Miles caught Suzanne's hand eagerly in his.

'Will you come out with me tomorrow?' he asked.

Tante Jeannette drifted tactfully past as Suzanne felt able to speak without reserve.

'I was hoping you would ask me,' she said frankly with a smile. 'There's so much that I haven't seen and it's so nice to have a guide who's seen it all before. Like you, my time here is short. I plan to return home to London fairly soon.'

He squeezed her hand with a look of not quite believing his luck.

'Good,' he said. 'I have a short session with Raoul first thing in the morning, then the rest of the day is my own. Shall we say eleven o'clock?'

She nodded, watching him stride forward to join Tante Jeannette, patiently waiting to show him his room. What a boon it would be to get away from Raoul for a day, not to mention giving Tante Jeannette uninterrupted time with her beloved husband. On the way to her room her thoughts turned inevitably to Raoul.

How she had hated to see him stroll nonchalantly with Sylvana to her car! His deep chuckle had mingled with his companion's laughter at something he had said while he readjusted the fur cape around her shoulders. Futile to remind herself that he had learned to live without Suzanne Dawson, that he had fallen in love with someone else.

Maybe after a day away from him she would be able to recover some of her resilience; at least, she could become more reconciled to the fact that she had lost him for ever. It would not prevent her from loving him. The awful ache inside her had to be lived with until she had come to terms with it.

In her room she undressed slowly, with a strange reluctance to go to bed to toss and turn. The tap on the door came as she stood in her briefs and bra. Thinking it was Tante Jeannette she said, 'Come in,' before reaching for her wrap. Then the wrap fell from her fingers as she turned, hearing the door open and close. The heat rushed to her cheeks, leaving them burning hot.

'Don't look so embarrassed,' drawled Raoul. 'It isn't the first time I've seen you in a state of undress. We lived together—remember?'

The cool front she had maintained since meeting him again, the tremendous battle fought between her treacherous heart and her head, all the resolutions she had made concerning his magnetic influence and deadly charm, all crumbled in one fell swoop as he leaned back against the closed door to regard her with the old mockery.

'Allow me,' he murmured, moving forward across the room from the door to sweep up her wrap before she could do anything about it.

In the inevitable silence that followed Suzanne eyed him balefully before pushing her arms inside the wrap he was holding at the ready. The brief respite gave her time to steady her voice.

'Since I have no man in the room I hardly think you've come to remind me of that,' she said bitingly.

He watched her tie the belt round the wrap and his eyes wandered slowly over her flushed face, the hair turning to molten gold in the wall lights, the deep blue depths of her eyes, and the slight figure.

Leaning back against the dressing table, he spoke with narrowed gaze.

'I thought I would call to ask you what you are doing tomorrow. Miles is here for a few days and I thought we could make a party up, four of us—Miles, you, Sylvana and myself.'

He eyed her enigmatically as she wrapped the ends of the belt around her fingers, and gradually a smile lifted the corners of his well cut mouth.

'Don't get too excited, will you? I can assure you that you will enjoy every minute of our day,' he said sardonically.

Suzanne could not bear to look at him. She felt quite wretched and at the mercy of her muddled thoughts. The temptation to go out with him even in the company of Sylvana and Miles was strong, even though it meant grasping at something that could never be. Raoul was in love with Sylvana and there would be the torture of seeing them together.

Her eyes lowered, she said in a low voice, 'I'm going out with Miles.'

The straight dark brows lifted. 'He's certainly lost no time,' he said. 'Has he told you about the girl in Jersey? He put a call through to her before leaving the airport this evening.'

Suzanne bit her lip, still refusing to raise her eyes. 'Miles hasn't had much time to tell me anything, has he? In any case he's only here for a few days, and I shall soon be leaving myself.'

Raoul frowned heavily as she raised her eyes. 'Why are you leaving so soon? You haven't had time to see the island properly. Why this sudden decision?'

'It isn't a sudden decision. Now that Oncle Philippe has come home I can hardly intrude upon their privacy.'

'Nonsense!' he exclaimed roughly. 'They are both very fond of you and they will be very upset if you leave before your time is up. I understood you would be staying for a month or so?'

She met his eyes steadily. 'I've changed my mind. Tante Jeannette will understand. After all, the invitation was given twelve months ago when I was abroad.'

'I'm well aware of that,' he answered. 'What's more, I think that there is some other reason why you are leaving so soon.'

'I don't think my movements have anything to do with you,' she told him.

His next words brought her heart up to her throat. 'Are you leaving because of me?'

Her lips trembled. 'Why should you say that? I didn't come here because of you, so why should I leave for that reason?'

He looked at her keenly and she lowered her eyes. Her heart was beating fit to choke her. The very thought that he had guessed her true feelings for him made her cringe inwardly. She was getting too hypersensitive for words—he could not possibly know about her love for him.

'Quite possible,' he argued. 'You make no secret of your dislike for me. However, I'm sure you can forget all about it for one day. We can have a day to remember. I've never seen a place quite like Hong Kong for entertainment. Sylvana, I know, will enjoy it.'

Sylvana, she thought bitterly. Only Sylvana mattered where he was concerned. But then Sylvana was fun to be with. Suzanne Dawson was not much fun these days. She had changed. But Raoul had not; he was as strong and indomitable as ever. Suzanne stared down at the carpet, not wanting to see the deep intenseness of his dark eyes, the dark crisp hair, the mobile mouth that could curl upwards so endearingly.

She said rather weakly, 'I don't think you ought to be here in my room, do you? It's ... late.'

He laughed. 'You know, Suzanne, you have changed. A year ago you would have ordered me out.'

'Perhaps I've learned the futility of ordering you to do anything,' she retorted. 'You wouldn't have left then, and I'm sure you won't now unless it suits you.'

'Yes, you certainly have changed.' He leaned forward to touch her cheek with the backs of his fingers. She drew back as if she had been stung and his dark eyes hardened. 'Perhaps I ought to qualify that last remark. You haven't changed towards me. You still dislike me, do you not?'

Suzanne swung round and turned her back on him. 'Does it matter?'

'Of course it matters. I want to know what you've been doing this last twelve months and why it is that you can still dislike me after a period of neither seeing or hearing from me. We have had no time to talk up to now.'

She quivered inwardly as from an east wind. She thought, he's going to tell me he's going to marry Sylvana; he's that kind of man. Well, she had to face it some time.

In her utter unhappiness she turned and their eyes

met, locked. He had her completely baffled, this man who had once lived with her as her husband.

She looked away from him. 'You know as well as I do that we have nothing to discuss.'

'What do you plan to do when you return to London? Take a lover?'

She clenched her hands. 'If I do, I'm free to do so!'

'You know what I think?' he said, and went on before she could answer, 'You will go in search of a father figure who will spoil you like your father did. You are too afraid to fall in love. And do you know what? I prefer you as you were. At least you never bored me.'

Suzanne struck back. 'How fortunate for you then that we eventually parted! It would have been too dreadful if you'd been bored.'

He laughed suddenly. 'Here we are sparring—quite like old times, except that we shan't be in the same bed.'

Suzanne quivered. If only he knew how she longed to turn back the clock to when they were! Her heart gave a lurch. One step and she could have been in his arms.

She changed the subject. 'I could ask you how long you plan to stay in Hong Kong,' she said with an attempt at lightness.

'It depends,' he replied laconically.

'Upon Sylvana?'

'Perhaps.' Raoul spoke as if he wanted no discussion that involved Sylvana or himself.

Stung by the way he was locking her out of his affairs, she cried,

'For heaven's sake, you began this conversation. Aren't I permitted to ask questions about you?'

Raoul said coolly and without a deal of interest, 'What are you so worked up about? Naturally I am concerned with what you do with your life. You are not fitted to run your own affairs single-handed—your father saw to that.'

Suzanne shrivelled up. It was impossible to forget the feeling of being a trespasser on alien territory, her every move watched, weighed and found wanting. Now, with her hopeless love for him eating her heart out and adding to her other emotions, her mind was past thinking clearly.

Misery welling up inside her discharged itself on a derisive note.

'I'll keep you posted,' she cried insolently. 'Now will you please go? I'm tired.'

Without a backward look she went to the bathroom and closed the door. She was too tensed up to hear the door close as he went and the tears trickled down her working face.

With Raoul again resident in the house, it seemed to Suzanne that everything around was presented in a strong and more virile life-style. Awakening to sunlight and warmth, she realised that Raoul's personality was powerful enough to enrich everything around her. Listening to the birds in the curly-roofed eaves, she revelled in a feeling of being protected, free of all fear and hurt, although she knew it was sheer fantasy.

The feeling remained as she went to breakfast with Oncle Philippe and Tante Jeannette.

She met Sun Yu-Ren looking more immaculate than ever in his black silk trousers and white jacket, his black hair shining in the sunlight. His slanting eyes twinkled as they always did on seeing her.

'Good morning, missy,' he said politely. 'Beautiful day for everyone.'

She wondered if this charming little man was romantic too, for he was plainly delighted at Philippe's return—or was it Raoul's? She knew Raoul was his favourite, for he had not taken any pains to hide his admiration of her ex-husband. What his opinion of herself was she would never know, but he was always so nice to her and she knew she would miss him too when she had gone from this lovely house on the Peak.

Raoul and Miles had breakfasted earlier and were in Raoul's study, leaving the three of them to breakfast.

Oncle Philippe was easy to converse with. Like Raoul, charm flowed from him like oil pouring over troubled water. He teased Suzanne, complimented her on her appearance, and encouraged her mood of feeling protected and safe. But Suzanne felt awkward and alien with two people who needed only each other after so much time apart—so much so that by the time Raoul and Miles appeared she was more than ready to go with them for the day. To her surprise Raoul insisted upon her sitting beside him in the front seat of his big car, leaving Miles to sit in the back.

'You will see more of the island,' he explained. 'Which is one of the reasons for this outing.'

Suzanne climbed in, thankful that the roominess of the interior lessened the risk of any personal contact with him, even the casual touch of his arm as he leaned over to see that her door was safely locked.

They drove down from the Peak towards the town. Suzanne knew that every curve was taking them closer to picking up Sylvana. And as they drew nearer to the charming walled-in house and garden she heard Raoul laugh for the first time. It must have been at something Miles had said which she had missed in her rapt attention in the scenery. There was a reason for his gaiety; he was going to see Sylvana.

Seated there wretchedly beside him, Suzanne had been uneasily aware that the silence between them had been over-long despite the shortness of the journey. But she was too aware of her love for him—too afraid of saying the wrong thing.

Sylvana came out of the house and through the courtyard with her summer dress floating around her long slender legs. Bracelets gleamed on her honey-gold arms, her smile was infectious and if she resented her sitting beside Raoul, Sylvana did not show it.

At Sylvana's request they parked the big car with some vans in a walled garden belonging to a friend of Raoul's and went walking around the shops. Sylvana stopped several times for purchases and Suzanne was delighted to find herself outside the shop where she had been about to buy a present for Tante Jeannette on the day she had seen Alan going by with his white stick.

In her enthusiasm, she caught Raoul's arm. 'I want to go in here,' she said as Sylvana disappeared into a herbalist's next door.

Raoul lifted dark attractive brows. 'Come on, then. Anything special?'

He had put long fingers around her elbow and smiled down at her as they walked into the shop. Miles had paused to gaze in the window of the herbalist.

'I saw some very pretty jade,' she said, 'and I thought it would make an excellent present for Tante Jeannette. She's been so kind to me and I want to give her something nice.'

'It certainly will be nice from here. This is one of the few shops that deal in first-class jade and not your synthetic material.' Raoul greeted a tall slender man behind a glass display counter. 'Good morning, Mr Yee Lee. We would like to look at some jade.'

Suzanne said quickly, 'I saw a bracelet and matching earrings the other day when I was here. Have you still got them?'

'If we have not I am sure I can find something to please Missy.'

Suzanne watched the delicate ivory hands of the elderly shopkeeper curl lovingly around pieces of jade on display. Then he was placing them before her on the counter.

Mr Yee Lee shot a swift glance at Raoul before he said smoothly,

'It was the plain jade and not the jewelled kind, like this?'

He fingered a bracelet, on black velvet, of dragons that were intricately entwined and beautifully carved.

'That's right,' said Suzanne, picking up the tiny phoenix earrings.

'The jewelled set in the case behind you,' put in Raoul. 'May I see them?'

There was an instant's quietude as Mr Yee Lee laid the pieces of jade by the others on the showcase. The difference in the two sets was startling. The precious stones brought the carving into life. Suzanne had never seen anything like them for exquisite workmanship.

'Well? What do you think?'

Raoul was looking down at her, a rare and charming smile on his lips.

Her eagerness dimmed as she answered him as steadily as his direct yet impersonal gaze would permit.

'They're beautiful, of course.'

She wished she could have been natural with him, to slip a hand into the crook of his arm and smile up at him instead of being on her guard lest she should give her feelings away. And Mr Yee Lee was smiling on them benevolently as if he was pleased to give them so much pleasure.

The next moment two more jewelled pieces were displayed on the black velvet pad, a jade jewelled bracelet and ring.

'Your birth sign in jade,' said Raoul above her ear. As in a daze she felt him take her hand and slip on the ring.

'Very pretty,' said Mr Yee Lee. 'Could have sold it many times, only too small size. Many had tried it but not fit. It is a perfect fit for Missy. Make special concession.'

Raoul did what was expected of him and began to bargain for them. Suzanne slipped off the ring, and a price was reached which brought a smile to Mr Yee Lee's slanting eyes. While Raoul made out a cheque, the three sets of jade were packed into a small parcel which Raoul slipped into his pocket.

CHAPTER TEN

THE packet was waiting for Suzanne on the dressing table of her room when she went to dress that evening for dinner. She fingered the jade with the full knowledge of what she was going to do. The cheque covering the whole amount was in her handbag, and it was the work of a few minutes to get it and ring for Sun Yu-Ren to take it to Raoul's room, with a note.

The jewelled jade she would give to Tante Jeannette. The plain jade and the jewelled bracelet and ring she would give as presents to her friends when she returned to London. There were several with the same birthdate as herself. She wanted nothing to remind her of Raoul. Today had not been bad, though. Indeed, it had been a success as far as the four of them were concerned.

Before lunch they had gone round the shops, seeing, hearing and feeling the real aura of Hong Kong, the snake shops on Jervois Street and the egg shops in Wing Sing Street. Suzanne loved the atmosphere of courtesy and Oriental charm, and had ignored Raoul's sardonic grin at her wide-eyed wonder. Apart from herself they had seen it all before, and she could not help thinking how wonderful it would have been if she could have wandered around hand in hand with Raoul. But it was not to be. It was Sylvana who took his hand from time to time, and Suzanne had looked away with the numb feeling in her heart which was now commonplace.

After lunch they had gone to the Ocean Park in Aberdeen, one of the largest marine palaces in the world, to see the performances of the dolphins and sea-lions in the Ocean Theatre. Suzanne had loved it and Miles said,

'Your enthusiasm makes me feel jaded, Suzanne. I envy

you the freshness of gazing at things for the first time.'

Suzanne had laughed. Around them, as they drank the delicately flavoured tea and nibbled refreshments, the Ocean Park was something outside the modern world of pain and disillusionment. She had noticed Sylvana many times during the day, noticed how thoughtful she was at times in a withdrawn kind of way. She would take care not to lose Raoul when once she had him. Whereas Suzanne Dawson had known nothing about him beforehand Sylvana knew a great deal. She also knew how to get her man, something else that Suzanne Dawson had never bothered about.

Perhaps it was bearing this last in mind that made her choose to wear the lovely emerald, grey and black cheongsam. Surveying herself in the mirror as she smoothed the dress over her slender hips, Suzanne pondered on what jewellery to wear with it. The jewelled bracelet and ring would go with it beautifully, but nothing would persuade her to wear a gift from Raoul. All the same she could not resist taking them from their case and trying the effect.

A slow whistle from the direction of the door made her swing round to look into Raoul's mocking dark eyes. Negligently he leaned back against the closed door, and fleetingly she recollected the first time she had met him, tall and wide-shouldered with the white dinner jacket throwing the teak tan of his face into relief. For some reason her heart had begun to thud as it was thudding now. The bracelet dropped from her fingers on to the dressing table, and his dark eyes narrowed at the gesture.

'Having difficulty with the clasp?' he queried, coming further into the room. He was within a few feet of her when he paused to look her over with searching and hard eyes. 'And what,' he added, 'is the meaning of this?'

He waved the cheque she had sent to pay for the jade in front of her.

'To pay for the jade,' she answered in faint surprise. 'Surely you didn't think I'd inveigled you into the shop to pay for the present for Tante Jeannette? We could hardly argue in front of the owner of the shop, could we?'

'I ought to ram this down your throat,' he said darkly as he tore it up into small pieces and flung them disdainfully into a nearby waste paper basket.

'Why don't you?' she replied sweetly. 'Then I shall have an excuse to ram the jade down yours.'

His nostrils thinned and a corner of his well-defined mouth pulled in slightly.

'Don't try me too far,' he threatened. 'Now let's have no more nonsense.'

Picking the jade bracelet from the dressing table, he draped it around her wrist and she felt his cool fingers against her skin as he fastened it.

'There,' he said acidly. 'You don't deserve to look so lovely.'

To her chagrin he took his time in looking her over, and she gave him a look of utter disdain.

'Satisfied?' she asked, her hands clenched by her sides.

Raoul studied her as if she was some kind of mathematical problem, then he smiled. 'Not exactly,' he drawled.

Reaching out for the jade ring, he picked up her hand. For moments Suzanne kept it clenched, then slowly she opened her fingers. He slipped the ring on and she quivered inwardly, remembering another ring which was locked away, had been since the divorce was made absolute.

He said softly, 'Look on the present as a gift for your twenty-first birthday. Forget it is from me and enjoy it.' He held her fingers in his warm hand. 'Such small, pretty hands, just made for rings.'

Suzanne snatched her hand away in an effort to control her treacherous heart which had always responded to his touch from their first meeting.

She said angrily, 'I wish you would stop treating me like one of your lady friends! I'm not!'

Raoul raised a dark brow. 'That is the last thing I regard you as.' The dark eyes glinted devilishly. 'Any of my lady friends would have rewarded me with a kiss had I made them such a gift. I never expected one from you.'

She saw the glint and trembled. She cried passionately, 'Why did you have to be here in Hong Kong?'

'My dear girl, I conduct a part of our business from here. Why should my presence here upset you?'

'It ... it isn't your presence entirely.'

She lowered her gaze, finding his intent look too disturbing.

'What is it, then?' he insisted. 'Because I made you a present of the jade?'

'No,' she replied frankly, 'it's you yourself. You are ...' She broke off to search for words, seeking inspiration from the jade ring on her finger, but the jewels in it seemed to mock her.

'Yes?' he prompted maddeningly. 'Go on.'

'You're far too maddeningly and completely sure of yourself. You're too ... too ...'

'Masculine? You mean I am a constant reminder of what you are missing in the way of masculine companionship? I am not too insensitive to realise that you always had your father's and that you must be missing him dreadfully. On the other hand, I could not in any sense of the word regard my own relationship with you as fatherly.' His shrug was very French. 'On the other hand, I wonder what exactly you miss—a father's loving care or a husband's?'

'I haven't analysed my feelings. I'm not your kind of woman, otherwise you wouldn't ask such personal questions.' Suzanne's voice was as normal as she could make it beneath his probing gaze. 'I don't suppose you ask Sylvana such questions. But then she would know, wouldn't she? She's more sensible than I am. Her feet are kept firmly on the ground, unlike mine.'

Raoul agreed. 'Yes, Sylvana is not in the least like you. But we are not discussing Sylvana, are we? To go back to what I was saying. Since I take it that you miss your father the most let's pretend that he's given you the bracelet and ring.'

He moved in still closer and, before she could draw back, a firm finger was placed beneath her chin and he was gently forcing up her face. His impersonation of her father's voice was very good.

'Here you are, my darling, your birthday present with all my love,' he said.

The next moment he had hauled her into his arms to imprison her lips with his. His mouth was hard, warm and demanding, and Suzanne was shaken with shock and delight. The inevitable followed, a mounting panic. Exerting every bit of her strength against him, she felt his hold relax.

'Very funny,' she said shakily.

His mouth was amused but his eyes were steady and serious. 'Are you hating me so much, Suzanne?' he asked, seeing the tears spring to her blue eyes.

She drew away with a dignity that sat well on her youthful, slender shoulders.

'There you go again,' she said with an attempt at lightness. 'Always asking personal questions.' She looked at him fleetingly. 'As a mere acquaintance you have no right to ask such questions.'

'You are right, of course.' A pause. 'But there is something between us that goes beyond the bounds of being merely acquainted. We do know each other intimately.' Another pause. 'Or have you forgotten?'

Her face was the colour of a red rose. 'How like you to remind me!' she retorted indignantly. 'That was part of my growing up, nothing more.'

He took his time looking her over, taking in the gleaming golden hair, the deep blue eyes, the lovely slender column of her throat and the Chinese dress which she wore as seductively and enchantingly as any Oriental girl.

Then he smiled faintly. 'I have no argument there,' he said with irony. 'You certainly made a good job of it. You could not have done it in a more delightful way. May I say how well the dress suits you?'

She felt a sudden glow that warmed her heart. 'Thank

you, Raoul,' she said quietly. 'And thank you for the birthday gift. I still want to pay for Tante Jeannette's present.'

'Never give up, do you?' He glanced at his wrist watch.
'Heavens, look at the time! I must go and fetch Sylvana—
her car is out of commission. See you later.' At the door he
looked back and grinned. 'Your lipstick is all smudged. I
would hate Sylvana to see it—she could get the wrong
impression.'

He was gone, leaving Suzanne with an emotion that was
mixed with jealousy. She repaired her lipstick and slowly
recovered from the bitter-sweet experience of being
thoroughly kissed by Raoul. As if it was not enough to be
under the same roof! At least he was unaware of her love
for him. But then he was in love with Sylvana. That
rankled. Not that she could blame either of them for the
unhappy position she now found herself in, but it did look
as if a nightmare was pending for her upon Raoul returning with Sylvana.

Returning her lipstick to its case, she put it down on the
dressing table and stared down at it unseeingly for quite
some time. She felt numb, yet her pulse was beating fairly
quickly. Silly really for her to feel so shattered because
Raoul had kissed her. There had been no passion in his
embrace, no affection in the kiss.

Even an affair with Miles would not touch him as far as
she was concerned, neither would her departure from Hong
Kong. Suzanne put the jewelled jade bracelet and earrings
into her evening purse to give to Tante Jeannette, and
resolved to make plans for her departure. There was no
point in staying on to torture herself with the sight of
Raoul and Sylvana together.

Jeannette and Philippe were already in the salon with
Miles, who greeted her with flattering eagerness. In true
French tradition, Philippe poured her an aperitif and eyed
her with appraisal while Jeannette patted the vacant seat
beside her on the sofa.

She said admiringly, 'How lovely you look, *ma chère*. I like the jade bracelet and ring—they go beautifully with your very pretty cheongsam. Come, sit down beside me and tell me what you have been doing today. I trust that Raoul did not wear you out with sightseeing. He is so indefatigable!'

Suzanne sought safety in a smiling rejoinder as she sat down to receive her drink from Philippe. She hoped her companion would not ask about the bracelet and ring since she felt that Jeannette would not approve of her nephew buying gifts for his ex-wife.

'I've had a lovely day,' she answered lightly. 'I have a present for you which I hope you will accept for being so kind in inviting me here.'

'A present? For me? Surely not?' Jeannette cried in surprise, and Suzanne thought she looked a little embarrassed.

Her gasp of delight, however as she opened the small packet more than made up for her strangeness. The jewelled bracelet and earrings went well with Jeannette's hitherto unadorned dress in oyster silk. Philippe and Miles came across the room to admire the gift and in that moment Raoul arrived with Sylvana.

Sylvana had dressed as though aware of the competition of her friends. Her festive harlequin-print caftan in lightweight pure wool was eye-catching and she looked radiant. Watching her graceful entrance, Suzanne thought with a faint tremor that one could not blame Raoul for falling in love with her. They were placed next to each other at the dining table with Suzanne facing them beside Miles.

Sylvana was more talkative than ever this evening and her colour was high, giving the impression that she was excited about something. Despite her determination to ignore their presence by giving her attention to Miles, Suzanne found her gaze straying across to where they sat. Once she had to look away quickly when Raoul placed a hand gently over Sylvana's on the table. Agitation set her heart racing. Thoughts tortured her. Had he spoken of his love to her earlier in his car as they had driven back to the house when he had collected her?

After dinner, a telephone call took Raoul out of the room and he returned to ask Jeannette, Philippe and Miles to accompany him to his study, leaving Suzanne alone with Sylvana.

Sylvana said as they moved to the terrace together, 'Did you know that Jeannette and Philippe plan to return to Paris quite soon?'

Suzanne said carefully, 'Yes. I shall be moving on myself any day. What about you?'

Sylvana did not reply for a moment. Then she said, 'I am going to Paris also.'

'With Raoul?' Suzanne had spoken on an indrawn breath and waited tense for the reply.

'We shall probably all go together.' Another pause, then, 'You are in love with Raoul, aren't you, Suzanne?'

She turned to look at Suzanne's face, pale as a magnolia in the fading summer night, and followed her to stand to look over the bay, shrouded now in mist with lights springing up all over the place.

'You are in love with him, aren't you?' Sylvana insisted.

'Yes—I love him, but I'd die if he were to find out. You must never tell him. Promise, please, Sylvana!'

'Why did you have to come to Hong Kong?' Sylvana cried passionately. 'Why? Could you not have seen that meeting Raoul again after all this time would only lead to heartbreak for you? Raoul is in love with me. After all, we have both been through a divorce. Raoul will be happy with me. Why should he not? We love each other. He loves me —really loves me, I think. Why else should he seek my company? And you have seen how happy we are together.'

Suzanne nodded. 'You're right, of course. I ... I've been in love with Raoul for a long time and I didn't come here to try to get him back, you know.'

'It does not matter to me one way or the other, *cara* Suzanne. Jeannette and I are already very close, and mar-

riage to Raoul will cement that friendship. Raoul will be
delighted because of it. I'm sorry that things have turned
out like this for you, honestly I am, but you cannot put
back the clock. You must see that it is hopeless for you to
remain here now that Jeannette has her husband back. I
have known of your love for Raoul for some time.'

Suzanne drew in a sharp breath of apprehension. 'Is it so
obvious?' she cried.

'Only to me, I think, because I happen to be in love with
him myself. And let us face it—you are not only very lovely
in every way, you are also younger than I am, much
younger. I must confess that you have given me many uneasy moments.'

Suzanne was contrite. 'I'm sorry, Sylvana. I didn't mean
to cause you or anyone else any unhappiness,' she said. And
then more gently, 'You see, I never expected to see Raoul
here in Hong Kong. I came with the intention of keeping
Tante Jeannette company until Oncle Philippe came back.'

Sylvana said quietly, 'Don't upset yourself over what has
happened. I have enjoyed your company. You and I might
have been very good friends had we met in other circumstances. It is only for your own sake that I am telling you
to forget Raoul as he has forgotten you. It is hopeless, *cara*
Suzanne. There is no future in it for you. I am going to
marry him because the barrier of religion that I erected
between us is no longer there. At last I have accepted the
fact that my love for him is even stronger than my religious
beliefs.' She laughed as though at something remembered.
'Why, the first time we met, we were, how you say?—or as
Raoul would say—*en rapport.*'

Suzanne flinched inwardly as from a mortal blow. Her
face was flushed now, her silky hair windblown. She pushed
the silken strands away from her hot cheeks. All Sylvana
had said was true. Raoul had learned to live without her.
He had not even noticed that she had given Tante Jeannette
the gift of jade which he had paid for. Well, she would put
a cheque in his room before she left and make him accept

it. As for the set of plain jade, she would give that to Sylvana later.

By now Sylvana had lost her seriousness. She was bright and really interested again in her surroundings.

'Isn't it just too lovely here?' she said. 'I shall miss all this when I go.'

'Me too,' agreed Suzanne. Discussing Hong Kong and all its wonder was a safe topic now that an impasse had been reached between them. Towards the top of the Peak lights were springing into view among the pine trees from villas perched precariously on the slopes amid wreaths of mist. Soon she would be leaving this lovely place, hoping to take only the happy memories with her, like the day they had all spent together.

There was nothing for it but to go back and start again. She had to remould her life, this time with something positive. Before she had filled it with any kind of activity with nothing concrete as a result, certain that in the end she would blot out any aching memories of Raoul. And then just as her confidence was growing in her ability to do so, she had walked literally into his arms again, arms that she had hungered for.

She was more or less composed when the others joined them. Raoul said from somewhere near her shoulder, 'What about going up to the Peak to see a floor show and dance?'

It was Tante Jeannette who answered. 'You young people go. Philippe and I will enjoy ourselves listening to music.'

'Come on, Suzanne,' cried Sylvana. 'You will need a wrap. I brought one with me.'

Suzanne went to her room with mixed feelings. The last thing she wanted was to go anywhere with Raoul in the company. It was becoming increasingly difficult to hide her feelings from those keen dark eyes. Besides, no one was fooled by his suggestion that they go to the top of the Peak. He was feeling a little frustrated at not having Sylvana to himself and this was the only way he could do it. They would probably wander off together on their own, or dance cheek to cheek. Pain stabbed deeply into Suzanne's heart. What further proof did she need that he loved Sylvana, since he had never been a very gregarious person. Like Jeannette and Philippe, he was the kind to enjoy a quiet evening at home listening to music and he had never been particularly fond of dancing.

She took the first wrap that came to hand in the wardrobe, the little nylon fur jacket, and draped it around her slim shoulders. Raoul was even now at that very moment doing the same for Sylvana and she would be gazing up at him with laughter in her dark eyes. Lucky Sylvana!

Sylvana was already seated in the front seat of Raoul's car when she went out to join them. Miles was seated in the back seat and Raoul was leaning nonchalantly against the car when she approached.

Anger against his obvious indifference to her welled up inside her. But as she drew nearer to meet that intent dark gaze she felt his nearness like a pain. Her love for him swamped all else and she quickly lowered her eyes in case they betrayed her. He was smiling in a sardonic way as he silently opened the door of the car for her to slide in the back beside Miles.

The road to the top of the Peak was very steep and, at times, the skyscraper hotels seemed to be tilting at an alarming angle. The view at the top was fantastic. Suzanne found herself standing between Miles and Raoul with Sylvana on Raoul's other side. Her shoulder was close to his arm and her skin prickled. But he was talking to Sylvana. Miles spoke to her and she answered only vaguely, aware of what she had let herself in for.

The place was fairly crowded as they made their way to the restaurant and ballroom. Right away Sylvana caught Raoul's hand and said, 'Let's dance.'

Suzanne and Miles followed them on to the dance floor. Miles danced well and at any other time Suzanne would have enjoyed it as she tried to relax. They danced for a while, mingling with the crowd, and Suzanne tried hard to lose herself in the music. Miles talked about the changes in the island as they danced and she answered in monosyllables. Once Raoul passed them with Sylvana in his arms and Suzanne knew that she would be haunted by the sight of them together all her life. Other pictures—Raoul talking to Sylvana, laughing with her, taking her hand, and bending that dark head of his in the charming way he had to give his whole attention to what she was saying. She wanted the music to go on for a long time before meeting them again.

All too soon the music ceased and there was Raoul making his way towards them with Sylvana.

Coolly, he said, 'A change of partners is called for, I think.'

Suzanne felt herself drawn into his arms as the music began again and he swept her off among the dancers.

'Enjoying yourself?' he asked when several moments had elapsed.

'Immensely,' she answered as he drew her still closer to protect her from another rather boisterous couple heading their way. 'You've changed. You used not to prefer going out to spending an evening at home. In fact, if I remember correctly you were never much for tripping the light fantastic.'

'True,' he answered. 'People change.'

'So they do,' she agreed, and almost breathed a sigh of relief as his grip on her slackened again into the conventional hold. He was so heartbreakingly close that she felt sick with longing for him to lower his head and put his tanned cheek against her flushed one.

'Feeling tired?' he asked after a short pause.

'Not really. Why do you ask?'

'Because I miss that glow you exuded on the dance floor.'

'As you say, people change. I still love dancing.'

'You mean when you're not dancing with me?'

She laughed softly and was surprised how well she did it. 'Why should you say that? You're one of the best dancers I've ever known, and I knew some good ones,' she said frankly.

And it was true, she told herself wryly. He had an inborn ease of movement, giving the impression that all his muscles moved in a synchronisation of complete relaxation. It was an essential part of his charm, the almost feline grace of being nonchalant yet ready to leap into movement at the drop of a hat.

'*Merci*,' he murmured sardonically. 'I trust that remark means a softening in your attitude towards me. May I chalk that one good point up in my favour?'

For some reason Suzanne could not refrain from smiling. 'I wasn't aware that we were keeping a scoreboard!'

'It helps sometimes in the game of life. Incidentally, you are just like a scrap of thistledown. You want to eat more, *ma chère*. I still have a notion that you are pining for a lost love.'

Suzanne missed a step, apologised and righted herself. Raoul was moving his hand over her back and she stiffened in a vain effort to prevent her smothered desires from materialising. She was on dangerous ground in more ways than one. The thing was to play it cool.

'You have changed,' she said. 'Quite the romantic, aren't you? Sylvana must be a very remarkable girl. Raoul de Brécourt the cynic, now a romantic!'

He tightened his hold on her fingers. 'What has Sylvana to do with it?'

'She's softened you up. You must be very fond of her.'

'Sylvana is quite a girl,' he answered laconically. 'We were talking about you earlier.'

A chill feathered across her skin. She said frigidly, 'You were discussing me with Sylvana?'

'No, *ma chère*.' He gazed down mockingly into her up-turned wide blue glance. 'We are all returning to Paris very soon. And you are coming with us.'

'And Sylvana?' she asked in a voice strangely unlike her own.

'Yes,' he answered, and offered no explanation. 'We shall all be going except Miles, who is returning to London.'

The dance number was nearing the end and Suzanne spoke quickly.

'I shan't be going to Paris. I shall be going back to London.'

His lips thinned. 'I expected you to be awkward,' he said grimly. 'Look, if you are thinking along the lines that you will be in the way, forget it. We all want you to come.'

Aware that he was moving towards a door, Suzanne said, 'That's very kind of you, but I have other plans.'

The music throbbed to a close and he grasped her arm to take her through the door near to them.

'May I ask what those plans are?' He was leading her to a small table beneath a colourful awning with a panoramic view of the peaks of Kowloon. Pushing her down on to the nearest of the two chairs, he lowered his long length into the other and added, 'Has Miles anything to do with your plans?'

Suzanne spoke huskily, avoiding his eyes. 'Has Sylvana anything to do with yours?'

'Sylvana will be in Paris. She is very fond of you and could be a good friend. It hasn't escaped the notice of us all how lost and defeated you have looked since coming to Hong Kong. Who knows? Paris could be what you need at the moment.'

Suzanne curled up inside. To return to a city filled with memories of her honeymoon there was to her the last word in torture. It would be more than flesh and blood could stand to see Raoul arming Sylvana around all the places they had once visited hand in hand. He had treated her as a child then, as if taking the reins from her father for a short time.

Futile to feel hurt, she told herself. Her part in his life, whatever it had meant to him, was over. The wisest thing to do, since they were soon to part for ever, was to be as impersonal to him as he was to her. A few added pleasantries thrown in would help to relieve a situation which could very easily get out of hand.

Raoul had leaned back in his chair to place a long, lean brown hand on the table. It was near enough for her to reach out and place her own over it as he had done with Sylvana. What would he do if she did? Lose a little of his habitual calm in the embarrassment of receiving advances from an ex-wife he no longer wanted? In that moment Suzanne's pride was at its lowest ebb. She shivered, and instantly he was leaning around the side of the table to take her hand from her knee into his warm clasp.

'You are cold,' he said roughly. 'I'll fetch your wrap from the car.'

Left alone, she remained staring unseeingly at the view until Sylvana's voice aroused her.

'Where is Raoul?' she asked sharply.

Her dark eyes were rapier-sharp in their scrutiny of Suzanne's pale face. By now Suzanne had had more than enough. Her temples had begun to throb and she wanted to get away.

Standing up on shaky legs, she said, 'Raoul has gone to fetch my wrap from the car.'

'Don't you feel well?' Miles cut in with some concern. 'Shall I take you back to the house?'

Suzanne paused. If she looked half as sick as she felt then she looked awful, she thought with dismay. Her smile flickered, then grew brighter. It included them both.

'It's nothing really. I have a bad head. I think I would like to go back to the house, but I can easily get a taxi. I don't wish to spoil your enjoyment.'

'Poor Suzanne!' Sylvana purred, placing an arm around her. 'Miles will take you home, *mia cara*. I am sorry.'

Her arm dropped as Raoul returned with the little nylon jacket. He looked at them all keenly as he stepped forward to place it around Suzanne's shoulders. His fingers were cool against her neck as he adjusted it to fit her snugly.

'What about a drink to warm us up?' he suggested, and

regarded them in turn with a slight frown. 'Is anything the matter?'

Miles said, 'I'm taking Suzanne back to the house. She is not well. I can get a taxi.'

'Not well?' Raoul looked sharply at Suzanne's pale face. 'You did not say you were not well.' The dark eyes narrowed to frame a glitter in their depths, then he softened. 'We will all sit down and have a drink, then we will all go home. Please sit down, all of you.'

He put Suzanne back gently into her chair, drew up two more from a table nearby for Sylvana and Miles, then he left them.

Miles said, 'Raoul is right, Suzanne. A drink will warm you up and I for one would not say no. What about you, Sylvana?'

Sylvana shrugged. 'I don't mind.'

Suzanne said nothing and wished desperately that she had not come out that evening. She also felt terrible about spoiling the evening for the others. Raoul had gone away for the drinks tight-lipped and looking thoroughly fed up. She had spoiled his jaunt with Sylvana and she was sorry about that. His happiness was the most important thing to her now.

Sylvana had gone quiet, drumming her beautifully manicured fingers on the table with a look in her eyes which said she had made up her mind about something important. Then Raoul was back with four glasses of different coloured drinks. He handed them round, leaving Suzanne's and his own until the last. He put her glass into her hand, saying firmly,

'Drink every drop.'

Then he lifted his own glass, included them all in his rather tight smile and tossed it off. Suzanne hovered over hers, found the aroma from it pleasant and took a sip. It ran like fire down her throat and warmed her stomach. Miles and Sylvana drank theirs more slowly, Sylvana speculatively.

She said, 'May I have a cigarette, Raoul?'

Raoul slipped a case from his pocket, flicked it open and offered it to Sylvana. Then after offering Miles a cigarette, he put on a lighter.

Sylvana drew on her cigarette and flicked Suzanne an unreadable look. 'Have a cigarette, Suzanne. It will steady your nerves.'

Suzanne made no answer and Raoul made no move to offer her a cigarette, neither did he have one himself. They were too closely grouped around the table for Suzanne to relax. Raoul sitting next to her was much too close for her comfort and Sylvana, as usual, was making her presence felt only too keenly.

Miles said quietly after drawing contentedly from his cigarette,

'How are you feeling, Suzanne?'

Raoul leaned forward and lifted the hand cradling her drink to her lips. 'Drink up,' he commanded. 'Then you can tell us all how you feel.'

His fingers were warm and strong around hers, sending a kind of electric current up her arm as he forced the glass against her lips. She drank the rest of the sparkling liquid in three sips and only then when the glass was empty did Raoul withdraw his hold.

Her whole being suddenly seemed to be alight inside. Whether it was reaction to his nearness or to the drink Suzanne could not have said. Nevertheless her heart was still numb and she just had to get away.

'I feel fine,' she assured them, and pushed back the golden hair from her flushed face. As the colour came back in her cheeks she avoided Raoul's eyes. The music had begun again in the ballroom and Sylvana was tapping her foot impatiently. She looked appealingly at Raoul.

'Let's go for one more dance, Raoul,' she begged. 'It's early yet and I'm sure Miles won't mind taking Suzanne back to the house.'

Suzanne, not wanting to see the look of disappointment

on Raoul's face at the thought of taking them all home, added quickly, 'Yes, do go. I'll take a walk around the top to see the view. The air will be good for my head.'

Miles said goodhumouredly, 'I'll come with you—I'm not much for dancing anyway.'

So while Sylvana dragged Raoul away to the dance floor Suzanne strolled with Miles to breathe in the air.

'It's so fresh up here,' she cried, holding her face up to drink in the sweet hill air so free from the smell of joss-sticks, cooking and fumes that permeated the city below.

Miles gazed at the clear line of her profile and the youthful line of her slender throat.

'Why did you come to Hong Kong?' he asked suddenly.

Suzanne turned to fix him with a wide blue stare. Then slowly her expression changed.

'You know, don't you? You know about Raoul and me?' she whispered.

He nodded. 'Yes, I know. You're still in love with him, aren't you?'

She shook her head. 'No, not still in love with him. I am in love with him, but only since our divorce.' The words came out naturally before they were arrested by the look of horror on her face. Her hand flew to cover her mouth. 'Goodness!' she cried. 'If you've guessed that I love Raoul surely he must know too?'

He smiled. 'I'd say Raoul would be the last to know. No, I've been watching your reaction whenever he appeared. Out here you're an entirely different person from the one taking a drink five minutes ago at that table. I think Sylvana knows it too.'

Suzanne swallowed on a dry throat. 'Yes, she does. But she won't say anything to Raoul because she wants to marry him.'

'And does he want to marry her?'

'I think so. She's going with them to Paris.'

'I see. But don't you think you ought to make sure that Raoul does want to marry again?'

'I know he does. He told me not long ago that he had his future all planned out and it was nothing to do with staying on working indefinitely for the family concern.' Suzanne clenched her hands over the rail of the veranda. 'You ... you won't tell him what I've told you ... about loving him, will you? I'd die if you did. At least I have my pride left. Please let me keep that.'

Miles looked down at the earnest young face below his and smiled.

'My dear,' he said gently, 'I would never dream of such a thing. Raoul is the kind of man who wouldn't hesitate to tell a girl that he loved her, so perhaps you're right and he does love Sylvana. Mind you, I'd rather him than me. She's much too volatile, too explosive to make a cosy wife. I don't think I would keep any Ming vases in the establishment I shared with a woman like Sylvana.'

Suzanne said, 'You're only saying that to comfort me. But it doesn't, you know. I would hate to think of Raoul being unhappy. I would feel his unhappiness as I would my own.'

'That's very generous of you. Why don't you make sure of his happiness by going after him yourself?'

She shook her head. 'One can't make a person love to order. Raoul is in love with Sylvana, so that's an end of it.' She gave him a sad smile. 'I'm resigned to it now. It hurt terribly at first knowing that Raoul was lost to me for ever. I suppose it will always hurt.'

Miles said unexpectedly, 'I knew your father. He gave me the chance to be where I am today by introducing me to a friend of his with business in the city.'

Suzanne looked up at him with soft lips parted. Her eyes shone.

'You knew my father?'

He smiled. 'He was a fine man. I shall always be grateful to him for what he taught me—Raoul too. He's a fine young man, you know. I don't think your father would have given up so easily.'

'You mean Raoul? There's no point, is there? He doesn't love me—he never did.'

He looked at her in frank disbelief. 'My dear girl, if you know anything at all about Raoul you would know that he would never marry for gain.'

'My father's company and Raoul's were merging. Wouldn't you say that was reason enough?'

'You haven't much idea of your own attractions, have you? No man could be in your company long without noticing delightful things about you.'

Her lips quivered. 'Why are you being so kind to me? I've practically spoiled your evening.'

'On the contrary, I've had a delightful evening.' Miles paused, then added, 'By the way, I'm leaving for London tomorrow afternoon.'

Suzanne looked at him in dismay. 'So soon?'

'Afraid so.'

She bit her lip and wondered how to phrase her next words. 'Do you think I could go back with you ... on the same plane, I mean? Tante Jeannette only asked me here to keep her company while Oncle Philippe was away. Now he's come back I'm sure she'll be relieved to be rid of me. Besides,' she gave an unhappy little laugh, 'as Raoul's ex-wife I'm only an embarrassment to them.'

'You mean you feel you're in the way? But you're here by invitation.' Miles spoke slowly as if giving the matter some thought. 'What would you have done if I hadn't been here?'

'Left just the same. Going with you will make it easier. For some reason Raoul thinks I need someone to look after me. He certainly won't have any objection to my leaving with you.'

Reasonably, he said, 'Raoul booked my seat back. You could ask him to get you a seat on the same plane. After all, there's no need for any secrecy. If he agrees I shall be delighted to take you back with me.'

'I'll ask him,' she said, and her blue eyes were pleading.

'You won't mention anything of our conversation to him, will you? What I've told you is in confidence. I've never said anything to anyone about my love for Raoul, not even Tante Jeannette. He must never know.'

'I understand,' he said gravely. 'I give you my word.'

But when Raoul and Sylvana joined them later, Suzanne knew what she was going to do, and that included acting on her own without saying anything to Raoul at all. For one thing she was too upset at the thought of the emptiness facing her in her life ahead once she had said her final goodbye to Raoul. By the morning she would not be feeling so bad.

Sylvana was quiet on the way down the Peak and Miles did not say much. Perhaps they were waiting for a lead from Raoul, who was quiet also. He put on speed and soon they were arriving at the house. It was well past midnight and all was quiet. Jeannette and Philippe had gone to bed and Sun Yu-Ren had left a covered tray for them in the salon. Raoul asked Sylvana in before he took her home, and Suzanne, refusing refreshment, went to bed.

She undressed with the knowledge that Raoul and Sylvana were downstairs together, Miles having gone to bed after also refusing refreshment. Earlier at the Peak when Raoul and Sylvana had joined them on the veranda, they had appeared hand in hand, Sylvana her usual radiant self.

'I've enjoyed myself immensely,' she said. 'You ought to have brought me here more often, Raoul. What about coming up again before we leave for Paris? Jeannette and Philippe can come with us. They would love it.'

Raoul had looked at her teasingly. 'We'll see,' he had promised. 'How's the head, Suzanne?'

His voice had become impersonal even to the using of her name, she thought, and managed to reply in a similar vein. He had given her one keen look before they had all gone to his car.

Suzanne had undressed and put on her nightdress when

she missed the jewelled jade bracelet from her wrist. Thinking that she had already taken it off and put it down somewhere absentmindedly, she searched all the surfaces in the room, beginning with the dressing table, but it was nowhere to be found. Where on earth could she have dropped it? Could it be in the car, having fallen from her wrist on the way back to the house, or had she lost it in the restaurant on the Peak?

Her intention to get rid of it was blown sky high by the fact that it was Raoul's last gift to her, and it became very important indeed that she should find it. Hastily shrugging herself into her housecoat she belted it and went in search of a telephone directory for the number of the restaurant on the Peak. On her way she met Sun Yu-Ren coming out of the main salon with the tray. Raoul and Sylvana had evidently had a night cap and gone.

In a few hurried words she asked Sun Yu-Ren for the number of the restaurant on the Peak and rang them up. No bracelet had been found, but they would look for it making a thorough search when the guests had gone, they told her. On returning to her room Suzanne was unable to rest. She had no reason to believe that the bracelet had been lost at the restaurant, or indeed in the car.

In any case, was it not the best thing to happen? Another bond broken between her and Raoul before the final one. Her head argued one thing, her heart another. In the end, Suzanne left her room to go to the garage. Raoul had had ample time by now to take Sylvana home and return. The house was quiet when she made her way outdoors where lanterns still illuminated the courtyard and the gardens.

Raoul's car was there in the garage. She had no torch, but it did not take long to feel around the back seat and the floor. Nothing there. Disappointed, Suzanne made her way slowly back through the courtyard. The moon was out, turning the acacias into beautifully modelled waxed-petalled beauty. Her head had been down, intently examining every inch of ground, when something suddenly alerted her.

Raoul was standing in the shade of the acacias near to the entrance to the house. His face, the lean dark features topped by a rich cap of black hair, looked more chiselled than ever. Suzanne, taken unawares, retreated a little. Disconcerted, she raised a hand to her face, suppressing any deep emotion his appearance usually brought in its wake. He had just returned from seeing Sylvana home; her perfume, still in the car, teased her nostrils with the memory of it. Raoul was perhaps remembering it too, along with her kisses. Already the emptiness of her life ahead was all around her. Inside she was just a hollow shell.

He heaved what sounded like a sigh of relief. 'For the moment I thought you might be walking in your sleep. Sorry I startled you. The air is too keen for you to walk around in a housecoat,' he said.

He came forward slowly with the moonlight turning dusk into a cold light. Cold as her heart, she thought, and she said hurriedly, 'I was just coming in.'

Somehow he was standing in front of her, barring her way, and all the time she had kept her eyes upon his dark, controlled, expressionless face.

'Your hair is like silver in the moonlight and your eyes are deep blue pools of apprehension. Dangerous thing, wandering about in the early hours,' he murmured softly.

'I agree, and I'm rather tired.'

'Tired of me, you mean? I did linger here knowing that you would appear. I watched you go to my car.'

'You did what?' Righteous indignation tore at her throat. 'You've been spying on me?'

Raoul shrugged. 'I knew what you were looking for—this.'

He drew something from the pocket of his evening jacket, the jade bracelet, and held it up. The jewels in it caught the light.

'But ... but where did you find it, and why didn't you give it to me?' she cried angrily.

'I intend to,' he answered equably. 'When we have had our little talk.'

'What little talk? What can we possibly have to say to each other?'

'You could go out with me tomorrow after lunch. Miles is leaving then. We could take him to the airport and go on somewhere quiet. As you probably know, we are returning to Paris and letting someone else take over the reins.'

'And what's that to do with me?'

'You hold a certain amount of shares in the company,' he reminded her with such icy deliberation that Suzanne felt herself freezing up inside.

'So you want me to sell out to you? Is that it?'

'Not necessarily.'

'What, then?'

He said, 'I wish you would not persist in treating me as an enemy. Why not call a truce and come out with me tomorrow?'

Suzanne clung on to clear thinking. One did not have to be very bright to see that he had talked the whole thing over with Sylvana and she had suggested him making a clean break from his ex-wife by buying her out of the company. To be truthful, Suzanne had forgotten about her shares in the de Brécourt empire. She had not even touched the alimony allotted to her.

Her voice was a trifle shaky, but hurt made it hard. 'Don't worry—I shall see my solicitor when I return to London. You can have the shares gratis. Think what a nice wedding present they'll make for Sylvana.'

She moved swiftly around where he stood and fled indoors before the tears not far away spilled over. She heard him call her name and realised that he had not given her the bracelet. Well, he was welcome to it! She would throw in the ring for good measure, another present for Sylvana. She dragged off her housecoat and climbed into bed to review the fact that her marriage to Raoul was truly at an end. All that was needed now to sever the last thread binding them together was a rustle of paper, her signature for the disposal of her shares in the de Brécourt empire—or was it the transfer? Who cared? Not Suzanne Dawson. But the slow trickle of tears between her lashes was saying something very different. If only Raoul had not discussed her with Sylvana! To her way of thinking that was the unkindest cut of all.

CHAPTER ELEVEN

LIFE had to go on even when one had lost the taste for it—so thought Suzanne on awakening next morning. She had the confused feeling of not enjoying deep restful sleep. During the night she had drifted into light sleep, only to awaken at intervals because her dreams were anxiously given over to Raoul and their eventual parting. She left her bed, deciding that the day was to be one of action. First her clothes would have to be packed. Then she would telephone the airport for a seat on the afternoon plane out of Hong Kong.

Sun Yu-Ren bought her tea and when he had gone she opened her cases and began to pack. She put her soiled linen out to be laundered as usual and left the toilet things on her dressing table and in the bathroom to avoid comment. Everything had to be done as discreetly as possible.

She telephoned the airport before going to breakfast and was told that owing to a cancellation there was a seat available for her that afternoon to London. So far so good. The thing was to go and collect the ticket, just in case, after breakfast.

To her relief there was no one in the dining area of the salon to greet her. Sun Yu-Ren told her that Raoul and Miles were talking business having breakfasted in the study. Jeannette and Philippe did not put in an appearance and Suzanne deduced that they would probably be joining the two men later in Raoul's study.

The day was misty with a fine rain falling, but Sun Yu-Ren's smile was as bright as ever as he served her with breakfast. Suzanne did not linger. After breakfast she tripped lightly to her room to put on a mackintosh in white waterproof cotton which she belted tightly around her trim

172

waist and tied a pretty scarf over her hair. Once the plane
ticket was in her possession she would begin to relax.

She picked up her shoulder bag and turned to meet the
sweet air coming in through the window. Looking back on
her first days here at this lovely house on the Peak, she told
herself that the most sensible thing to have done would have
been to leave directly she knew that Raoul was involved
with Sylvana. That way it might have been possible to have
eventually put them both out of her mind. Her only excuse
was that her love for Raoul was far stronger than her pride
or pain. And she was partly responsible for Raoul being
free to marry again.

Scarves of mist shrouded the view over the islands. But it
was good clean air and the gentle fine rain was not unpleasant, mingling as it did with the tang of the sea. Turning up the collar of her mackintosh, she turned and left the
room. On the way to the front door she cannoned into
Raoul hurrying back to his study with a sheaf of papers
in his hand.

He looked tall, lean and sardonic in a cream summer
weight suit. With the thick black hair curling in tidy
tendrils about his neat ears and sunburned neck, and his
dark eyes appraising her mockingly, he was typically
French.

'Going out in the rain?' he asked with a lift of a dark
brow, a mannerism that never failed to set her pulses racing.

Her blood quickened. 'Yes.' Her smile was meant to dis-
arm. 'It's good for the complexion.'

His eyes roved over her complexion glowing clear and
smooth as a child's, her lips pinkly fresh, and the willowy
figure chic and smart in the white mackintosh.

'Going far?' he queried, tapping the papers in his hand
against the open palm of the other.

Suzanne had tried hard not to look surprised and dismayed at meeting him, and she quivered inwardly, remembering that he had never missed a trick in the past.

The mesmeric quality of his gaze combined with his personality was almost her undoing. But not quite.

She did the only thing under the circumstances. She laughed, a pleasing little tinkle that made light of the situation before he made something of her sudden departure.

'Taking a breath of air,' she said.

His eyes narrowed and he stopped tapping his palm with the papers.

'Suppose you go to sit in my car,' he said evenly. 'I'll be with you in about five minutes to take you where you want to go.'

Coolly he took her silence for consent and with a charming smile he turned on his heel to leave her staring after him.

'You'll be lucky,' she muttered under her breath, and made for the door.

The mantle of fine rain enveloping her and hanging on to her eyelashes had a sobering effect on her. She was still trembling after the chance encounter with Raoul and her face burned. Fortunately she had a lift right to the airport from a young couple who were on their way there. They had been on their honeymoon, and were now on their way home. They had hired the car and it was to be picked up by the firm on their arrival at the airport.

They were an ordinary young couple in their early twenties and there was a glow about them; but then, Suzanne reflected, they were very much in love. The young man was so proud of his wife, and the girl was drowned in happiness. Some of that happiness rubbed off on Suzanne as she left them at the airport to go to reception to pick up her ticket.

'You're lucky,' said the girl who attended to her. 'The plane leaves at three this afternoon.'

The rain had stopped when Suzanne eventually reached the town to do some last-minute shopping. One thing she liked about Hong Kong was the young people. There ap-

peared to be a surfeit of them. The women were so deliciously feminine, from the young things with their long
black hair and lovely figures to the older beauties, some of
whom were elegantly attired in the glamorous cheongsams
with their provocative side splits. They were a friendly
race, and one small boy with almond eyes and a fringe of
black hair cut almost level right around his head held up
his kite to show her as she wended her way through the
crowds.

Shopping was fun, or nearly so, since it would be the last
time she would be visiting the shops. Among her purchases
were several delightful cheongsams, and a Chinese silk
dressing gown for Oncle Philippe with lots of happy young
dragons printed on it in discreet colours. Suzanne had
hesitated between the brown silk and the wine colour when
the shopkeeper said with a twinkle, 'Dragons protect. Very
friendly. Nice present for husband or number one uncle.'

She picked up the brown one. 'For number one uncle,'
she said with a smile.

He held up the wine-coloured one, said softly, hopefully,
'For number two uncle?'

Suzanne paused and admired the beautiful quality of the
Chinese silk. Dragons protect, he had said, and the two
words held a poignant meaning that brought a lump to her
throat. In the end she bought it for Raoul with the intention
of leaving it for him on her departure that afternoon.

Time had passed quicker than she had realised, and on
consulting her wristwatch, Suzanne found she just had
time to call to say goodbye to Sylvana and to give her the
plain jade bracelet and earrings she had originally chosen
for Jeannette before hurrying back to lunch at the Peak.

But Sylvana was out. Leaving the present with the daily
woman, Suzanne paused as she walked again through the
charming courtyard and looked back at the house in silent
prayer. Be kind to Raoul, please, she said, and closed the
gate.

A feeling of flatness assailed her as she set off for the

tram to the Peak. The sun was out now in force and she steamed beneath the mackintosh, but it did not seem to matter. She dragged the scarf from her hair with one hand while balancing her parcels with the other and was aware of the Rolls drawing up almost silently beside her.

'So we find you at last,' said Raoul, opening the car door and reaching out a long arm. 'Give me your parcels and hop in.'

He took her parcels and dropped them on the seat beside him, leaving her ample room in the rest of the spacious seat. Suzanne slid inside and was instantly aware of Miles sharing the back seat with Sylvana. She was conscious also of her dishevelled appearance, her shiny face damp with perspiration and her flattened hair. Tired and dispirited though she was, she still cared what she looked like when she met Raoul. She had been prepared to meet him at lunch time, but now her heart was thudding in an alarming way as he started the car.

He was silent for a moment, then, 'Why on earth didn't you wait and come out with us? Miles wanted to do some last-minute shopping and you could have come with us.'

She heard herself saying, 'I had to hurry to pick up an air ticket. I'm travelling back with Miles this afternoon.' She turned in her seat to flash a bright smile at Miles. 'I was lucky to get a cancelled seat.'

There was a sudden silence. Suzanne did not dare to look at Raoul because she had done the unpardonable thing where he was concerned: she had shown him how much she thought of his interference in her affairs. At least her pride had been saved. It had been left to her to cut yet another tie between them.

Sylvana said, on a note of surprise, 'I'm sure Miles will be delighted to have a travelling companion. Rather sudden, is it not, this decision to leave the island?'

'When did you decide to leave?' queried Raoul, as if he did not care one way or the other. 'Do let us know the reason. We are intrigued.'

Suzanne moistened dry lips. 'It isn't a sudden decision. I've been thinking about it since Oncle Philippe returned. I shan't be needed here now since you're all returning to Paris so soon.'

'You might have let us know,' Raoul said curtly as he set the car purring up the incline towards the Peak. 'Or do I happen to be one of those you have not told?'

Suzanne managed a small laugh. 'Of course not. I acted quickly because the opportunity of having someone to travel with was too good to miss. Tante Jeannette will understand.'

Suzanne having made her little speech, then addressed Sylvana to tell her about calling at her house to find her out. She made no mention of the present she had left but went on to say how grateful she was for all her kindness to her.

Suzanne always regarded the next hour or so as a time she would much prefer to forget. Raoul had put on speed and had reached the house as though he had not a second to lose. It hurt dreadfully to know that he could not wait to get her out of Hong Kong and his life. Unhappily, she carried her parcels to her room and did the last of her packing, marvelling as she did so at the speed with which the soiled linen she had put out that morning had been freshly laundered.

She wrote a note to Raoul along with a second cheque to pay for the jade and laid them on the dressing gown she had bought for him. The note was brief, thanking him for all he had done for her and wishing him happiness with Sylvana. She would be well on her way when they were found in her room. Oncle Philippe was delighted with his dressing gown and Tante Jeannette took the news of her sudden departure calmly. She made Suzanne promise to visit them sometime in Paris, but both knew that nothing would come of it.

Sun Yu-Ren had prepared a lunch filled with culinary delights, and his usual bright smile was missing when Suzanne kissed him goodbye. Even the cheque she surreptitiously pushed into his hand failed to bring him to his usual sunny self. Sylvana did not accompany them to the airport because Raoul had a business appointment after he had dropped them off there.

Suzanne wondered if it had something to do with his departure to Paris. He had put her beside him in the car, leaving Miles to take the back seat along with his briefcase and loose coat. So near to him and so very far away! All the way to the airport he was intent upon getting them there in the shortest possible time—something that puzzled Suzanne since he had been the one to insist upon them leaving early. Consequently there was plenty of time before their plane left. Why he should show such concern she would never know, because he was acting completely out of character. To see the unshakeable, nonchalant Raoul de Brécourt getting almost into a flap over catching a plane was something that disturbed her greatly. It only showed how anxious he was to be rid of her.

How bitterly she regretted coming now to Hong Kong. She had tortured herself and hurt Raoul. Yet there was a measure of comfort to be gained. At least she knew now that everything was over between them, no more vague hoping, no more wishing for a miracle that would bring them together again.

As the airport came in sight Suzanne felt her nerves tighten. She would have preferred having to run to catch the plane and so cut short an embarrassed leavetaking of Raoul. How would he react to a kiss? Oh no, not that! She could not bear it. One swift glance at his face told her nothing as he swung the big car to a halt. He had seemed to have gone back to his usual calm self as he turned towards her.

With no change of expression he said, 'Stay where you are for a moment while I get the cases out. I want to speak to you.'

Miles was out of the car and taking the suitcases while Suzanne sat waiting, and for several minutes she tried to assume some degree of calm. Then Raoul was sliding back into his seat and as he swerved the car around she had a glimpse of Miles standing there smiling with his case. Raoul turned briefly as he set the car off at speed and she received the shock of his determined gaze. His silence was subtle torture. Everything had been said and done between them, so why this little journey for what could only be some privacy?

'Where are we going?' she asked, seeing his reason for rushing them to the airport so quickly.

'Somewhere to talk,' he answered laconically.

Knowing him, she decided to let him have his way, but her nerves tightened. Since meeting him on her arrival in Hong Kong she had been terrified of him getting her entirely to herself in the mood he was in. With Raoul anything might happen. Since discovering her love for him Suzanne knew how easy it would be for her to become wax in his hands if she once allowed herself to surrender to that love.

At the speed he was putting on it soon became obvious that he was making for the road to the Peak. In silence she felt the car climbing past skyscraper hotels, then villas and gardens on to the hills. In a daze she watched him slow down to bring the Rolls to a halt on a layby. Then he opened his door and came round to let her out.

'I don't want to miss my plane,' she reminded him.

Raoul said nothing, but his look was less determined. His firm mouth even quirked a little.

For once Suzanne had no interest in the breathtaking view as he led her to a rough grassy hollow facing the sea which held the sun like cupped hands.

Perhaps he felt her quiver as he pushed her down gently on to the dry grass, for he said quietly, 'No reason to tremble. I am not going to hurt you in any way. Just relax.'

He flung himself down beside her, and Suzanne fixed her eyes on a magpie not far away nosing among the casuarinas and orchid trees. Had he been referring to physical violence? she thought grimly. Did he not know that words could be more lethal? One could recover from physical injuries, but hurtful words seared the memory for ever.

He had reclined on one elbow to stare out to sea and her restless hand toyed with the sparse dry grass. It occurred to her then that within a few hours she would be en route for London, and doing her utmost to forget Hong Kong. The sea, golden and gleaming, hurt her eyes; it was as good an excuse as any for the tears in them. This was to be her last scene with him, crying out for the need of a mask to hide her true feelings. Why then was he so slow in starting it?

'What did you bring me up here for? Couldn't you have told me what you had in mind at the airport or even in the house before we left? Why did you bring me up here, Raoul?'

She had spoken without looking at him, not wanting to weaken at the sight of those features which did so much to her heart. His eyes narrowed against the glare but he did not look at her.

'Perhaps I wanted a few honest answers to questions. Also I wanted to see what had happened to you since we parted without being hemmed in by curious glances. Are you happy, Suzanne?'

'Is anyone ever really happy?' she answered. 'The world is an alien place when one's closest relatives have gone.'

'What about relatives by marriage?'

She drew in a shaky breath of pure sweet air and felt the sun warming her limbs.

'You mean Tante Jeannette? She has been very kind to me and I like her very much.'

'Then why did you not consent to come to Paris with us?'

He looked at her sharply, eyes narrowed against the glare. His voice was sharpened by curiosity, not concern.

'Because I had made other plans.'

'Plans which you made after you were invited to Paris. Is that not so?'

It was a harsh, peremptory question and she resented it. 'I'm a free agent,' she cried indignantly. 'You have no right to question my movements!'

'I am only trying to get at the truth.' Raoul spoke with an aloofness that put their conversation on an impersonal footing. He no longer cared for her, but he wanted no skeletons popping out of the de Brécourt cupboards to mar his second marriage.

Her heart lurched. 'What truth?' The knowledge that the eggshell defences she had built between them could crumble at any moment weighed heavily upon her. 'Why not some truths from you for a change?'

He was silent for a moment, then he said, 'Such as?'

Despairingly, she cried, 'What does it matter? It's all so long ago. I shall miss my plane, and you have a business appointment.'

Raoul gripped her wrist as she struggled to free herself. 'What are these truths you want to hear from me?' he said grimly. 'Come on, out with it.'

By now Suzanne was tottering on the brink of something like hysteria. Flung from such emotional heights, and loving him as she did, she was in no state to reason. What was happening now was beyond all reason. She had followed the dictates of her heart which she knew with bitter humiliation she was capable of following against every vestige of her pride.

'Forget it,' she cried. 'We both married for the wrong reasons—I because my father wanted me to marry you, you because it was a business arrangement between two companies.'

He looked startled. 'Indeed? This is news to me. But let it pass. How do you feel about marriage now? You were too young before, in more ways than one.' He smiled grimly. 'You certainly fooled me!'

She said passionately, 'Raoul de Brécourt taken in by a woman? That will be the day!'

'Not a woman, *ma chère*. A girl,' he corrected her. Here was the mocking Raoul of old whom she had told herself she hated. He went on,

'So apologies are called for, would you not agree. Mine because I married you, yours because you married me?'

His voice had altered. As always it was laconic, but Suzanne sensed that he was being over-protective by making it very much easier for her to take the same line. Only she could not, because she now loved him desperately, whereas he had never loved her.

'I ... I can't apologise,' she began, wishing her voice would not wobble so much each time she began to speak. 'You would have married me in any case whatever I felt about you.'

'True,' he admitted with a self-derisory smile in his voice as he continued. 'But for an entirely different reason than the one you had for marrying me. I loved you. I thought that by leading you into marriage gently and a little platonically I would soon make you succumb to my charms and be all for it. Being a gentleman I handled you with kid gloves. I lost hold of the fact that to break in a young inexperienced filly, especially a well-bred one, one has to be cruel to be kind.' He smiled as though the thought pleased him and Suzanne looked quickly away. 'Now if I had behaved like that young cad I rescued you from I might have got somewhere.'

But Suzanne was not listening. She had stopped when he had told her that he had loved her. All she could think about was that she had killed that love. No use telling him now that it had worked; that what she had regarded as a marriage of convenience had been, in reality, the real thing for her; that she had only discovered it when it was too late.

There were all kinds of excuses she could have used had Raoul admitted to still loving her. But he did not, not now. So all she could whisper was, 'I'm sorry things didn't work out. And now perhaps I can go to catch my plane.'

He released her wrist, numb from his grip, but it was not as numb as her heart.

The next moment he had her by the shoulders and the gleam in his dark eyes made her heart lurch.

'You are not thinking of going without kissing me good-bye, are you?'

He spoke softly, dangerously forcing her on her back to gaze up at him in fear and trembling. For a long moment his head was bent over her, the dark face shadowed. Then slowly his head shut out the light. The next few moments were the most esctatic of her life. His kiss, beginning with a firm pressure of his lips, deepened slowly in passion and forced her own to respond. The blood sang wildly through her veins as he gathered her closer. Her heart said, this is what love means, this agony of joy in the arms of the beloved.

Gone was all pride, all resolution never to succumb to his charms. All that mattered was Raoul, who was holding her against his heart, close, fiercely loving. Her hands moved to clasp his back as she gave herself up to his kisses with an equal passion which surprised her.

'You have changed,' he said.

Suzanne knew her eyes were shining like stars as she hastily replenished her lungs. 'In what way?'

'You know in what way.'

Her face went scarlet, but her gaze did not waver. Slowly she came down to earth and the shadows were back in her eyes. 'I think we ought to go now, don't you?'

His gaze narrowed. 'Just as you wish,' he replied, and made a move to help her to her feet.

Suzanne walked blindly with him to his car. His kisses still burned on her lips, but he had forgotten all about hem. With his usual nonchalant ease of manner he helped her into the big car, slid in beside her and hastily opened a window to let in some air. The interior was hot, but Suzanne scarcely noticed it.

The descent from the Peak was swift, but instead of

making for the airport Raoul pulled up outside what looked
like an office block. Turning to her, he smiled for the first
time.

'Come on,' he said. 'We are right on time.'

Suzanne could only think of one thing: he wanted her
to sign the documents concerning her shares in the company in front of witnesses. He was taking no chances. As
usual he was having everything in order, which now meant
tying up the loose ends.

She felt her colour go at his callousness, or was it so bad
of him? After all, they were divorced. There was no reason
for her to hang on to the shares, and he was only being
sensible about it.

'You mean you want me to sign some documents?'

'That is right.'

Only the greatest self-control on her part made her smile
possible. With his hand beneath her elbow Raoul guided
her into the building, where he tapped on a door and
entered. Suzanne had kept her eyes down and lifted them
as they entered the room.

The man who rose from behind the desk put on half-
moon glasses and gave them a beaming smile.

With a polite bow, he said, 'Madame and Monsieur de
Brécourt, this is indeed a pleasure. Shall we begin?'

He rang a bell on his desk and bent down to sort out
some papers in front of him. Suzanne, thinking it strange
not to be asked to sit down, looked up at Raoul for the first
time. He smiled down at her with a look in his eyes which
she had thought never to see again.

He whispered, 'This is it, *ma chère*. We are about to be
married again.'

The next few minutes passed in a dream for Suzanne.
Two witnesses appeared, a man and woman who were obviously members of the staff. Suzanne was presented with
a bouquet of flowers and the service began. It was not until
Raoul slipped the eternity ring he had bought for the occasion on her finger that Suzanne began to be sure that she

was not dreaming. The kiss he gave her after the ceremony would surely have awakened her if she had been.

Back in the car she said with tears in her eyes, 'Was it so obvious that I loved you, Raoul?'

He laughed. 'If I was ever in any doubt I knew when I kissed you. You do love me, don't you?' He tossed her a swift loving glance.

'I love you more than anything else in the world. I was dying by inches all the way to the airport because I was sure I was leaving you for ever,' she assured him. 'I'll make it up to you for being what I was before Father died.'

'Hmm.' His swift glance brought the colour to her cheeks. 'You certainly have a lot to make up for, *ma mie.*'

They talked in sweet intimacy as they drove away, slowly now. The knowledge that they had taken their vows twice, and that they were sure of their love for each other, was in both their thoughts. They stopped at a café to celebrate, and Raoul slipped away from their table to make a telephone call.

Coming back to their table, he said. 'Time enough to go back home to the Peak for dinner this evening.'

They sipped champagne and tried to do justice to the vintage, but they were soon on their way again in the car. Raoul had to stop several times to kiss her happy face, and when they had disentangled for the umpteenth time, he said, 'Do you know, I've no idea where we are supposed to be going. Where would you like to spend the afternoon, *ma chère*?'

Eyes bright and lips tremulous, Suzanne said. 'Let's leave the car and just walk hand in hand. I really can't believe it yet. And there's so much I don't understand. Sylvana, for instance. Will she be very hurt?'

'About us, you mean? Why should she? There was never anything more between us than good friendship. She needed me for a while and perhaps I needed her company too. Did you know that she is going to Paris to study art? She has rented a studio there. I think she will return to

Italy eventually. In Paris she will miss the sun.'

'And Tante Jeannette?'

'I asked her to invite you to Hong Kong in the first place. You will never know what it meant to me to wait for you to come for twelve whole months. The time I have been away from you has been an eternity. I stayed at my club when you came in order not to embarrass you. I never slept between your arrival and discovering if you had met some-one else.'

He caught her to him and buried his face in her hair and Suzanne stared over his shoulder, remembering.

'But you agreed to a divorce,' she said. 'Just like that.'

'I came to see you about it, but you had gone on holiday abroad with friends. I did not seek you out because I hoped a final separation might bring you to your senses. You were beginning to care for me, although you did not know it. As I said before, I should have used strong-arm tactics—so be-ware, my sweet. From now on I mean business!'

Suzanne tried to untangle her thoughts, a herculean task clasped as she was against him.

'Are you sure about Sylvana? I think she is in love with you.'

Raoul released her a little and grinned down into her face. 'Were you jealous? I was hoping you would be. She was my only card to play against you. As for marrying her, it was out of the question. The barriers against it were of her own erection. I am not saying that they would have deterred me from marrying her if I had cared enough, but I did not.' He kissed the tip of her nose, and although his look was tender and loving, his dark eyes held pain. 'I wanted to come after you so much when we finally parted and you disappeared from the scene, but I was in the midst of important business commitments. Then as time went on without you I knew that nothing mattered to me if I had lost you.'

He had to kiss her again, the starry eyes bright with tears, the trembling mouth, the tender hand that caressed his dark face. Ardent moments passed. Raoul spoke of his jealousy

of Alan and Suzanne resolved to tell him at a later date all
about it. Nothing must spoil these precious moments from
life enriched with the magic of their reconciliation. They
had both gone through the furnace of experience and their
future life together would be all the more wonderful for it.

Much later Suzanne remembered the plane she was to
catch and Raoul informed her wickedly that it was never on
for her to go. He had cancelled her seat.

'If you had refused to remarry me I had planned to take
you off in some Chinese junk and keep you there until you
relented,' he said darkly.

Much later he drove back to the town and parked the car.
Then they strolled hand in hand, sublimely unconscious of
their surroundings. Raoul did point out a few places of
interest from time to time. They had tea in the grounds of
a Buddhist monastery where they laughed a lot and held
hands.

Steeped in bliss, Suzanne asked wistfully, 'Do we have to
go back for dinner at the house on the Peak? Couldn't we
stay here in town to keep this wonderful feeling of to-
getherness for just a little longer?'

'We shall be together, *mignonne*,' he assured her tenderly.
'We shall have the house on the Peak to ourselves.'

'You mean ... Tante Jeannette and Oncle Philippe have
gone?'

'That's right. They left for Paris at four o'clock this
afternoon. We shall follow them later when we have had a
week or two here on our second honeymoon—or should I
say our first real one?'

He laughed at her sudden deep colour and hugged her.
That night, at the house, they drank champagne with Sun
Yu-Ren, who beamed on them with delight. His slanting
dark eyes told them that it could not have happened to two
nicer people. They ate the wonderful meal he had prepared for them, then sat on the terrace in utter bliss to
savour their new-found happiness. Then Raoul closed the
French windows to shut out the world.

When he came into her room glowing from a shower his dark eyes deepened to find her there waiting for him looking sylph-like and palpitatingly lovely in flimsy négligé. Taking her hands, he kissed them with a sparkling vitality which had no need for murmured words to express what was in his heart. The eager surrender of her lips was all he wanted. As for Suzanne, words failed her. She still could not believe it. They were in bed when the last cloud of her unhappiness sailed away.

She placed her soft cheek against the masculine roughness of his, and whispered, 'Darling Raoul, I love you so much. I only wish that my father could know how happy I am.'

'Maybe he does, *mignonne*,' he answered against her lips as he drew her into his arms.

4 FREE

Harlequin Romances

Get all the latest books before they're sold out!

As a Harlequin subscriber you actually receive your personal copies of the latest Romances immediately after they come off the press, so you're sure of getting all 6 each month.

Cancel your subscription whenever you wish!

You don't have to buy any minimum number of books. Whenever you decide to stop your subscription just let us know and we'll cancel all further shipments.

Your FREE gift includes
- *Anne Hampson* — Beyond the Sweet Waters
- *Anne Mather* — The Arrogant Duke
- *Violet Winspear* — Cap Flamingo
- *Nerina Hilliard* — Teachers Must Learn